"I don't understand why we crashed."

"I think someone tampered with the brake line, made a small hole in it. Can you move? We need to get out of here."

Cash managed to pry his door open enough that he could get out. Then he ran around to her side, but it was no use. That part of the vehicle was up against the hill's incline. He hurried back to the driver's-side door. "I'm sorry, but you're going to need to crawl out this way."

Somehow, Jacy managed to lift herself up and over the center console, and finally out the door.

"Can you walk? The hotel isn't far."

"Of course." She let out a soft moan as she pushed away from the vehicle.

He slipped his arm around her waist. "Lean on me."

As they made their way back across the field, he raked his gaze over the area, searching for the perp who'd done this.

There was no sign of anyone, but he knew the assailant was out there somewhere.

And that person had just tried to kill them.

Laura Scott has always loved romance and read faith-based books by Grace Livingston Hill in her teenage years. She's thrilled to have been given the opportunity to retire from thirty-eight years of nursing to become a full-time author. Laura has published over thirty books for Love Inspired Suspense. She has two adult children and lives in Milwaukee, Wisconsin, with her husband of thirty-five years. Please visit Laura at laurascottbooks.com, as she loves to hear from her readers.

Books by Laura Scott

Love Inspired Suspense

Hiding in Plain Sight
Amish Holiday Vendetta
Deadly Amish Abduction
Tracked Through the Woods
Kidnapping Cold Case

Justice Seekers

Soldier's Christmas Secrets
Guarded by the Soldier
Wyoming Mountain Escape
Hiding His Holiday Witness
Rocky Mountain Standoff
Fugitive Hunt

Pacific Northwest K-9 Unit

Shielding the Baby

Visit the Author Profile page at LoveInspired.com for more titles.

KIDNAPPING COLD CASE

LAURA SCOTT

LOVE INSPIRED SUSPENSE
INSPIRATIONAL ROMANCE

LOVE INSPIRED® SUSPENSE
INSPIRATIONAL ROMANCE

Recycling programs
for this product may
not exist in your area.

ISBN-13: 978-1-335-59793-9

Kidnapping Cold Case

Love Inspired
22 Adelaide St. West, 41st Floor
Toronto, Ontario M5H 4E3, Canada
www.LoveInspired.com

Printed in U.S.A.

Yea, though I walk through the valley of the shadow of death, I will fear no evil: for thou art with me; thy rod and thy staff they comfort me.
—*Psalms* 23:4

This book is dedicated to my aunt Carolyn Wanke.
I am so blessed to have you in my life!

ONE

Another teenage girl was missing!

Forensic artist Jacy Urban huddled in her winter coat, casting a furtive look over her shoulder as she walked the ten blocks from the police precinct to her apartment building. The young girl's face that had been plastered all over the news in an Amber Alert was etched in her mind. Sixteen-year-old Suzanna Perry was pretty, athletic and blonde.

Just like Claire Simmons, who'd also gone missing three weeks ago.

Two young girls disappearing in the past month. This sort of thing didn't generally happen in Appleton, Wisconsin. Yet the similarities in these cases to the way she'd been nearly taken ten years ago brought forth a slew of memories better left buried.

A decade was a long time. No reason to think the same man was responsible for these two new missing persons cases after all this time.

Still, she couldn't help quickening her pace. As if the assailant who'd once grabbed her in Madison on her way home from choir practice had somehow known to find her here in Appleton.

Logical? Nope. But fear rarely made sense.

The attempted kidnapping and assault on her all those years ago had gotten her started in this path of being a forensic artist for the local police departments. She did freelance work for a dozen precincts within a hundred-mile radius, which kept her busy. She'd been dragged out of bed in the middle of the night or on weekends more times than she could count.

Truthfully, she didn't mind. Anything she could do to help put the bad guys behind bars was worth the inconvenience.

This evening she'd been called in at seven thirty to assist with identifying a burglary suspect. Since her car was in the garage for repairs, she'd walked to the precinct. It was eight thirty now, not too late. Yet the January darkness made it seem much later.

She told herself there was nothing to worry about. For one thing, she was hardly a teenager anymore. Additionally, she'd purposefully led a low-key, somewhat reclusive life after relocating here seven years ago.

Yet she really wished the guy who'd tried to kidnap and assault her back when she was sixteen had been found and imprisoned. Especially after three other young girls had gone missing. But no one had been arrested, making her wonder if the assailant had left town. Or if he'd been tossed in jail for some other crime.

A thudding noise startled her. She spun around, raking her gaze across the familiar neighborhood. A car door? Probably. Seeing nothing alarming, she drew in a shaky breath and continued walking. Her apartment was part of a square four-family building, two apartments on the ground floor and two upper units. She'd requested a second-floor apartment to avoid the possibility of someone breaking a window and crawling through to get to her.

Yep, even after all this time, she instinctively took protective measures to avoid becoming a victim.

Why hadn't she allowed Detective Vargas to drive her home? Pride had gotten in the way. That and her sheer determination not to act, think or behave like a victim.

When she saw her building, she let out a tiny sigh of relief and broke into a light jog, doing her best to avoid the scattered icy patches on the sidewalk.

Hurrying toward the front door, she frowned when she noticed the porch light had burned out. Making a mental note to let the manager know, she pulled out her keys.

Movement from the left caught the corner of her eye. She turned, instinctively falling into a fighting stance when she heard a spraying sound. It was so unexpected, she reacted too slowly to avoid the face full of pepper spray.

"No!" Fire burned in her eyes, making it impossible to see. Her throat closed, making her cough as tears rolled down her face. She waved her arms, hoping to strike the assailant as she screamed as loud as possible, which sounded more like a hoarse croak. *"Help!"*

"You're mine now, Jacy." The whisper sent shivers of fear down her spine. This wasn't a random attack, it was personal! A hand grabbed her arm, fingers digging painfully into her despite the winter coat.

"No! Help me!" She struck out with all her might, her fist managing to connect with her attacker's chin. She heard a muffled oomph, and struck again and again, desperate to get free.

The hand let go and stumbling sounds reached her ears, but she still couldn't see. Couldn't tell if her attacker was coming toward her again.

A frustrated sob rose in her throat. "Help! Please, help me!"

"Jacy!" A male voice reached her ears, different from the attacker's. Or was it?

She didn't know. "No, stay away! *Help!*" She shrieked as loud as she could, her burning eyes hampering her ability to get to safety. Being unable to see was horrifying, and she fully expected something hard to strike her at any moment.

"Jacy, I'm here." She reared away from the hand on her shoulder. "It's me, Cash Rawson. Do you remember me? I'm a police detective now, and I'm not going to hurt you. You're safe, Jacy."

"C-Cash?" She plastered herself against the front door of the apartment building, desperately wishing she could see the man in front of her. Was it really the nineteen-year-old who'd come to her rescue ten years ago? How? Why? Becoming temporarily blind seemed to have scrambled her brain. Her coughing eased a bit, but she still had trouble pushing the words through her constricted throat. "Did you…see who…did this?"

"No, and normally I'd run off to find him, but I won't leave you here alone." His voice was firm. "Let's get you inside. Are you okay?"

No, she wasn't okay. Who had blinded her with pepper spray? Who had tried to grab her? And why? "Why are…you here?"

"I came to find you." His voice was calm and soothing, much the way it had been when he'd found her at the bottom of a ravine ten years ago. "May I take your key? Help you inside? I promise you're safe now."

She swallowed hard, struggling to breathe normally. Her eyes burned worse than anything she'd ever imagined. No wonder so many cities had outlawed pepper spray. How long would it take for her vision to clear? Would the damage be permanent? She prayed not. How could she sketch if she couldn't see?

"Here," she said, holding the key up since she couldn't make out where he was.

"Thank you." She heard him unlock the front door and then put his hand beneath her arm. "Lean on me. I'll guide you inside."

Doing as he suggested, she allowed him to lead her. The burning in her throat was beginning to ease, but her eyes were still a mess. Shouldn't the tears help wash the spray away? "I'm on the—second floor." She turned toward the area where she was certain the stairs were located. Not that she could see anything but a dark blurry shape.

"Okay, easy now. We'll take the steps one at a time."

After helping her navigate the stairs, Cash used her keys to unlock her apartment. She felt along the hall then crossed to where her sofa should be. Shedding her coat, she tossed it aside and sat back on the cushion.

Without being asked, Cash set a box of tissues on her lap. She used several to blot at her face.

"You may want to shower," Cash said. "Rinsing with water is the best treatment for pepper spray."

"Did you do this?" she abruptly demanded.

"What? No, Jacy. I would never hurt you."

She wanted to believe him, but the timing of his

showing up so soon after the assault made her suspicious.

"I promise I didn't do this," he repeated. "I was at the police precinct, hoping to speak with you before you left. If you'd like to talk to Detective Vargas, he'll verify my story."

"Okay." Peering through her watery eyes, she eyed the blurred dark blob that she assumed was him. "I should wash up."

"Can you find the bathroom?" Cash asked.

"Yes." Her apartment wasn't that big. She blew her nose then stood and hesitantly made her way across the room. The full bathroom was next to her bedroom. She grabbed the discarded sweatshirt she'd been wearing earlier from the bed, taking it with her. Spray remnants stained her shirt and jacket.

As she gratefully washed away the aftermath of the pepper spray, her thoughts centered on Cash Rawson. Detective Cash Rawson.

Now that she was calmer, she knew Cash wouldn't have hit her with pepper spray. He'd have no reason to do such a thing. She was grateful he'd arrived when he had, interrupting whatever fate had awaited her at the hands of the assailant. Yet Cash showing up was no accident. He hadn't dropped in after all this time to check up on her.

No, she knew he'd come for one purpose.

To help find the missing teenage girls.

Who had attacked Jacy Urban? Cash paced the length of her apartment, peering out each of the windows to the street below. If he'd been even three minutes earlier, he might have caught the guy.

But leaving Jacy blinded and alone so he could search for the assailant had not been an option. Especially when there could have been more than one person involved.

The incident nagged at him for several reasons. The timing was the most suspicious. Two teenage girls had gone missing in the past three weeks.

And they were young, pretty and blonde. Just like Jacy.

Jacy had managed to escape her attacker ten years ago but had suffered a head injury as a result. He'd pulled over to the side of the road when he'd seen her running across the street and toward the woods. He'd jumped from the car and followed, finding her at the bottom of a steep ravine. At the time, she hadn't known her name, much less what had happened. Her memory had soon returned to the point she knew who she was, but could tell the police nothing about the events leading up to or involving her attack.

Or her assailant.

At nineteen, Cash had just graduated high school and hadn't been sure about his career path. A few days following Jacy's attack, especially after he'd sat with her while the police asked questions, he'd enrolled in a criminal justice degree program.

He'd earned his gold shield three years ago, and felt good about the investigations he'd done, bringing justice to those who had been hurt.

The moment the Claire Simmons case had hit the news, he'd noticed the similarities between her disappearance and Jacy's. Despite the decade time lapse between the attacks, he'd pulled the police investigation files about Jacy's case, along with the other missing girls' cases, poring over the details.

Then Suzanna Perry had gone missing.

And he'd had a very bad feeling the same thing was happening all over again. The same way it had ten years ago.

One small problem was that these recent disappearances happened in Appleton, not Madison, where he worked. Still there were three unsolved cases from ten years ago that he'd inherited when the detective who'd investigated them had retired. Three young girls who had disappeared after Jacy's attack. His boss thought he was chasing shadows coming here to Appleton. That the long-ago attack on Jacy could not possibly be related to what was happening now.

But Cash knew following his gut instincts is how he'd become a good detective. Refusing to let his boss drag him down, he'd driven to Appleton to meet with Vargas, who was kind enough to let him look at the files on Claire and Suzanna, then to speak with Jacy.

Who had hit her with pepper spray? It didn't feel like a teenage prank, but something sinister. As a way of hindering her ability to see her attacker.

Jacy finally emerged from the bathroom. Her chin-length blond hair was still damp, her eyes red and puffy from the irritant. But the way her green eyes zeroed in on him indicated she could see him. For the most part.

"How are you? Better?"

"You're still blurry, but the pain is better." She took a seat on the sofa. "Thanks for helping me."

"I wish I'd been here sooner." He sat on the opposite end of the sofa, leaving plenty of space between them. "I'm also sorry to drop in on you like this."

"You really spoke to Detective Vargas?"

"Yes. He sang your praises, by the way. Said you were instrumental in helping to close several cases."

She grimaced. "He's being nice. You must know that many departments are using computer programs to create likenesses rather than live forensic sketch artists. I'm fortunate to have precincts around here willing to utilize my services."

"Yeah, but those computer-generated models aren't nearly as good as you are. That's been showed time and time again. The ability of a sketch artist to work with the witness, tweaking small things, is worth every dime of your salary."

"Thanks." She twisted her fingers in the fleece of her sweatshirt, the only outward sign of her nervousness. Then she plucked more tissues from the box as her eyes were still watering a bit. "Okay, you may as well come clean, Cash. You didn't drive all this way for a friendly visit."

"No, I came because of the missing girls." He didn't add how much he'd thought about her over the years. How much he'd admired her. She'd come across as more mature than her sixteen years.

"I thought so." She sniffled, blew her nose, then shrugged. "I'm not sure I can help you. For one thing, the most recent disappearances were from a local high school here in Appleton. Do you have a new witness from Madison that you'd like me to work with?"

"I wish," he said with a heavy sigh. "No witness, other than you."

"Me?" She stared at him, blinking as if to bring him into focus. "What are you talking about? You know very well that I don't remember anything about the man who attacked me."

"I know that you didn't remember anything from ten years ago," he admitted. "But I thought these new attacks may have spurred a memory."

"Hearing about the missing girls has been devastating." Her voice was low and she dropped her eyes to her lap, her fingers crumpling the tissues into a tight ball. "There are no witnesses here or Vargas would have asked me to help sketch them. But as far as what happened ten years ago? You must know that if I had remembered anything, I would have called the police."

"I know." He swallowed a sigh, knowing this wasn't the time to ask what she did remember about the attack from ten years ago. He'd learned that sometimes victims remembered small details that they thought they'd already mentioned. "If you're feeling better, I'll drive you back to the police station so you can file a report about what happened here tonight. At the very least, they should increase police patrols to your neighborhood."

"I guess." She didn't move. "Did you see anything? Or hear what he said? He used my name, so this was definitely an attack against me personally."

He grimaced. "No, sorry. I saw a figure wearing black come toward you from the side of the apartment building. Next thing I knew, you screamed in pain. I was a block away. I ran as fast as I could and smelled the pepper spray when I arrived. Unfortunately, other than a person of average size and height, I didn't see anything more."

"Because the porch light was out." Jacy tucked her wet hair behind her ear. "I should have gone around back when I noticed that."

"I'm glad you didn't," he countered. "If I hadn't seen

you, I probably would have turned around and waited until morning to talk to you."

She frowned and nodded slowly. "I guess it worked out for the best."

"Do you have any idea why someone targeted you?" Cash wished he could take her hand to offer support. "Did you put a bad guy away recently?"

"I don't arrest people. But yes, two weeks ago I did a sketch that resulted in an arrest."

His pulse jumped. "Who? What's his name?"

"Her name is Felicia Gephardt. And she was arrested for armed robbery. She ripped off a series of gas stations."

"No camera footage?" he asked in surprise.

"She wore a mask—it's winter after all. Two of the three stations had cameras that were broken. The store owner of one of those thought she sounded familiar to a woman who'd come in a few days earlier when she wasn't wearing a mask. I worked with him to do a sketch, and that was enough for the police to find and arrest Felicia. They were able to connect her fingerprints to the other two gas stations." She lifted her gaze to his. "She's probably still in jail."

"You never know, someone could have posted bail for her." He rose to his feet and offered a hand. "Please, Jacy. Let's head back to the station and give all this information to Detective Vargas. He can find out if Felicia was the one who came after you tonight."

"Okay." After a very brief hesitation, she put her hand in his and allowed him to pull her upright. "Let's go."

He was relieved she'd agreed to his plan. Maybe he couldn't solve the cases of the missing girls, but he was hopeful that they'd get to the bottom of this recent attack on her.

It even made sense that someone had blinded her for sketching their likeness. Almost like a punishment for being able to draw well.

"Wait for me here. I'll pull my car up to the front curb." He'd parked farther down the road as there were No Parking signs in front of the two-story building.

"Sure." She managed a smile. Her eyes were still red and puffy, but she looked better.

As he jogged back down to the ground floor and out to his SUV, he knew the attack could have been much worse. People with severe asthma had been known to stop breathing entirely when being exposed to pepper spray. It was one of the reasons that buying it was restricted in some states.

But not in Wisconsin. Granted, their state law prohibited concentrations over ten percent, so this perp may have been illegally carrying. It was impossible to know how much Jacy had gotten, but he wouldn't be surprised if the concentration was higher than allowed by law.

A few minutes later, he pulled into the small visitor parking area in front of the precinct. He grabbed the door for her, then gestured for her to head inside.

"Jacy? Are you okay?" The man at the front desk greeted her with concern. Cash was glad the police knew her by name; it meant they'd take this assault seriously.

"I'm fine. Could we speak with Detective Vargas?"

"Sure thing." He unlocked the door so they could go back to where the detective was sitting at his desk.

Cash noticed Vargas hang up the phone when they entered. "Rawson? Jacy? What's going on?"

Jacy stepped forward and quickly described the recent attack. "I know pepper spray isn't a lethal weapon, but I got the sense it was used on purpose to blind me to make it easier to drag me away. He or she also said, 'You're mine now, Jacy' and tried to grab me. I managed to get free and call for help." She glanced at him. "Cash—er, Detective Rawson came running."

"Jacy's right. This was not a warped practical joke, but malicious intent," he confirmed.

Vargas took notes then sat back in his chair. "You think Felicia Gephardt is responsible?"

"I honestly don't know." Jacy frowned. "The voice was husky, but could have been a woman or a man. Isn't she still in jail?"

"I'll check." Vargas used his computer to access the criminal justice system. He grimaced. "Looks like she made bail and has another court date next week."

"Can you pick her up for questioning?" Cash knew the evidence against Gephardt was flimsy. As in nonexistent. "At the very least, you can figure out where she was tonight."

"I'll pay a visit to her last known address," Vargas agreed. "If she's not there, I'll issue a BOLO."

"Thanks." Then he thought of something. "How tall is she? The assailant I saw was probably five eight or five nine."

After glancing back at his computer, Vargas nodded. "She's five eight and weighs about one seventy-five."

"That's close to the same size and shape I saw." Cash hadn't had the impression the assailant was a woman, but then again, he hadn't gotten a clear look in the darkness. Bulky winter coats could also add pounds.

"We'll find her," Vargas assured them. He stood. "I'll walk you out."

Jacy was unusually quiet as they went back to Cash's SUV. "Are you sure you're okay?"

"Yes." She forced a smile that didn't reach her eyes. "I hope he finds Felicia and she admits to attacking me."

"But you don't think she did it."

"No, I don't." Jacy shrugged. "Mainly because of the whispered, 'You're mine now, Jacy.' Plus, the way he or she grabbed my arm, as if to pull me deeper into the shadows. I tried to fight, which helped, then you came running. But the real goal was to take me away."

He nodded in understanding. "I can spend the night on your sofa if that would make you feel better."

"That's not necessary," she quickly protested. "But thanks for the offer."

Cash drove her back to her apartment, once again pulling up directly in front of her building. Despite the No Parking signs, he wasn't going to let her walk alone. "I'll escort you up."

She didn't argue. Using her key, she accessed the main door and then headed up to the second floor.

She unlocked her apartment door, pushed it open and turned to him. "Thanks, Cash. Sorry I couldn't be more help."

"It's okay." He frowned and then grabbed her arm. "Wait. What's that on the floor?"

Jacy looked down then stumbled back toward him as if the item was a lethal snake rather than a sketch of a man's face with his eyes cruelly gouged out.

"Th-that's one of mine," she gasped.

"Yours? From where?" Cash didn't like the sound of this.

"I don't know. Maybe my portfolio in my apartment?"

Without hesitation, he pulled his weapon and pushed Jacy behind him. The assailant could be inside. Waiting for her!

TWO

Jacy gripped the back of Cash's jacket as he stepped inside her apartment. He used his foot to push the sketch out of the way, then swept his weapon from side to side, searching for the person who'd defaced it.

"Police! Throw down your weapons and come out with your hands on your head where I can see them!" Cash's authoritative demand was met with silence.

He moved quickly from room to room. Her portfolio was sitting on the end table in the living room, seemingly untouched. She swallowed hard, darting another glance toward the kitchen, half expecting to see one of her knives lying on the counter, having been used to gouge the eyes out of the man in her sketch.

But there was nothing. No indication the intruder had gotten inside. She should have felt reassured but didn't.

Cash took his time checking every hiding spot in her apartment, the closets and under the bed, before turning to face her. "We need to get you out of here, right now."

"Wait." Her pulse was racing, but Jacy didn't appreciate being bulldozed by him. "Let's just think about this for a minute. It doesn't look like anyone came inside. Otherwise why slide the sketch under the door?"

"Just because the perp didn't come inside, doesn't mean you aren't in danger."

"I know I'm in danger, Cash." She still had the burning red eyes and the bruises from the fingers grabbing her arm to prove it. "But who left the mangled copy of my sketch? The pepper spray assailant? And how did he or she get inside the building?"

"It would be a huge coincidence if the pepper spray attack was not linked to this drawing showing up under your door. Especially considering how the eyes were gouged out with something sharp." Cash scowled and walked over to pick up the sketch by the corner. He set it aside then added, "This perp is coming across as upset because you helped identify him."

"Yeah, I get that. But maybe the sketch itself is a clue." She sat on the sofa and opened her portfolio. While the finished pieces were now part of police files, these were drafts she kept for herself. Shifting through the sketches inside, she found the one she'd done years ago, one of the first she'd drawn for the Appleton police department. "The one I did is here." She held it up. "The damaged one is a copy. I wonder if his choosing this one is significant?"

"Who is he? The guy in the sketch?" Cash reluctantly dropped beside her on the sofa.

Having done hundreds of sketches over the course of her seven-year career, she didn't have them all memorized. But this one, she knew very well as he was her first successful arrest. "His name is Jonah King. He sexually assaulted two women at the Fox Valley technical college Appleton campus. He wasn't a student, the way his victims were. They helped me do this sketch, which in turn led to his arrest." She met Cash's gaze. "Maybe we should look into him, see if he's still in jail."

"I can do that." Cash stood and used his phone to make the call. After a few minutes, he returned. "King is still doing time, although he is up for parole by the end of the year."

"Parole? After sexually assaulting two women?" She shook her head in disgust. "That is so wrong."

"Doesn't mean the parole board will grant his release." Cash gestured to the drawing. "Where do you think this perp got his hands on this copy of your sketch?"

She slowly shook her head. "I'm not sure, especially since this was done so long ago. To be fair, copies were posted all over the city along with covering the entire campus in hopes of getting tips on his identity."

"You think there are copies up after all this time?" Cash asked.

"Maybe. Especially those placed around the college campus. It wouldn't surprise me if a few weren't taken down." Her brow knit, she tapped on the image. "I think the bigger question is whether Jonah King hired someone to come after me?"

"That's worth looking into," Cash agreed. He glanced around her apartment. "Okay, we need to contact Vargas to let him know about the sketch. And I'd like the document dusted for prints."

"That can be done tomorrow, no sense in bothering Detective Vargas now. The assailant is probably long gone."

"We hope he's long gone," Cash said dryly. "I still don't like the idea of you staying here."

She didn't want to admit she wasn't keen on sticking around, either. But it was her home, the only one she had. Since her parents' divorce and losing first one and then the other to different forms of cancer, she had done her best to make a life for herself.

And this creepy pepper spray assailant was not going to take that from her.

Cash sighed. "Okay, if you won't leave, then I'll stay, too. I'll sleep on your sofa," he quickly added when she arched a brow. "Please don't ask me to sleep in my car—it's too cold out there."

"Of course you can't sleep in your car." She grimaced then gave in. "I guess it's fine for you to sleep on the sofa. That way we can talk to the police first thing in the morning."

"Thank you." He made it sound like she was doing him a favor rather than it being the other way around. "I have an overnight bag and computer in the SUV. It will only take me a minute to grab them."

"Fine." She followed him to the door, doing her best to shake off her apprehension. The small landing outside her apartment was empty. Her neighbor was an older retired gentleman who didn't go out much. As Cash headed down the stairs to the ground floor, she closed her door and locked it.

Leaning her back against the door, she gnawed the inside of her lip while waiting for Cash to buzz the intercom to come back inside. There was no denying she'd feel better having him there. At least for tonight.

She wondered if the assailant was acting on behalf of Jonah King, or if this was the result of some other perp she'd helped put behind bars. It seemed odd that Jonah

King would send someone after her all these years later. More likely Felicia Gephardt was responsible.

You're mine now, Jacy.

The harsh whisper could have been from a man or a woman. When Cash hit the buzzer, the loud sound startled her so badly she thought her heart might burst from her chest.

Drawing in a steadying breath, she turned and hit the intercom. "Who is it?"

"Cash."

"Okay, come on in." She pressed the button to unlock the door then watched through the peephole until she saw Cash's familiar features. She let him in. "Hey." She frowned. "Why didn't you bring your stuff?"

"I saw a person lurking near the corner of the apartment building next door. I took off after him, but he got away." His expression turned grim. "We can't stay, Jacy. Not when this guy knows you're here. It's only a matter of time until the perp returns."

She shivered, the tiny hairs on the back of her neck lifting. "Fine. We can go." She hated knowing this guy was forcing her hand.

"I'm sorry," Cash murmured.

"Me, too." She forced herself to turn away, to pack a bag with a change of clothes, toiletries and, of course, her sketch book and colored pencils. At the last minute, she added her portfolio, unwilling to leave it behind.

She cast one last glance around her apartment, wondering when it would be safe enough to return.

If ever.

Normally, Cash would have carried Jacy's bag, but he decided it was better to hold his weapon at the ready.

While she'd packed, he'd placed the damaged sketch in a large plastic bag, hoping to get fingerprints from it. He tucked it into her bag, then stepped over the threshold into the hallway, waiting for Jacy to close and lock her apartment door.

"Stay behind me."

"Okay." She sounded breathless and he knew she was afraid.

With good reason. If he hadn't caught the barest hint of movement near the apartment building next to Jacy's, he might not have known about the assailant returning to finish what he'd started.

And that bothered him more than anything else. He needed to protect Jacy. He'd come to Appleton seeking her help, but now wondered if he'd somehow brought danger to her doorstep.

At the bottom of the stairs, he paused at the door to glance outside. He didn't see anyone lurking nearby and hoped he'd scared the assailant off long enough for them to get out of there.

Using his key fob, he unlocked the SUV. He glanced quickly over his shoulder. "Ready?"

Jacy gave a tense nod.

"Let's go." He pushed open the door, then held it for her. As she ducked through, he kept pace with her, blocking her body with his as much as possible as they quickly headed for the vehicle. He opened the passenger door for her then took her bag and tossed it in the back seat.

Less than a minute later, he was driving away from her apartment building. Jacy turned to look at him. "Where are we headed?"

"First, I'd like to drop the defaced sketch off at

the police station. I know they may not get around to checking for prints until morning, but I'd rather they keep the evidence." He shrugged. "After that, I'll find a hotel, preferably one outside the city with two adjoining rooms."

"I doubt they'll find fingerprints," Jacy said with a weary sigh. "The person who tried to grab me was wearing thin leather gloves."

"I know, but I have to try." Cash glanced at her. "You never know when a bad guy will make a mistake."

"I guess." She sounded exhausted.

"This won't take long. The evidence needs to be held secure in the police station, anyway." He tried to offer a reassuring smile. "We'll get to the hotel soon so you can get some rest."

"Rest." She shook her head. "Seems impossible. I keep trying to figure out how Felicia or anyone else would have gotten their hands on a copy of a sketch from six years ago."

"We need to make a master list of all of your old cases, check out which perps are still in jail and which ones may have gotten out recently."

"I don't remember them all," she protested.

"As many as you can," he amended. He understood her concern. He wouldn't be able to come up with a comprehensive list of perps he'd put behind bars, either. "And maybe those who are responsible for hurting others."

"Those are exactly the ones who should still be in jail, like Jonah King." She abruptly reached over to grab his arm. "Cash, what if this assailant has been following my career? Like, from the beginning?"

"That's possible." He hated the idea of someone

stalking her because of the police work she'd done. "But why would that same person come after you now? What triggered this most recent attack?"

"The missing girls?"

"You haven't worked on those cases."

"No." She sighed. "But only because no witnesses have come forward."

He pulled into the parking lot of the police station. Since it was late, he chose a spot right in front of the building. "I need a few minutes to drop off the evidence. Wait here."

"Yeah, sure." She forced a smile. "I hardly think an assailant is going to try something in front of a cop shop."

"Exactly." He twisted in his seat to open her bag and remove the plastic evidence bag holding the defaced sketch. "I won't be long."

Cash had to use the intercom to be let in since most police stations didn't have open lobby areas 24/7. That was just asking for trouble. He instructed the desk clerk to have the picture dusted for prints and to be given to Detective Vargas. "He can call Detective Cash Rawson for further information."

"Understood." The clerk labeled the bag. "Anything else?"

"No, thanks." He didn't waste any time in heading back outside, breathing a sigh of relief when he saw Jacy sitting calmly in the passenger seat.

He slid behind the wheel then used his GPS screen to find nearby hotels. "Here's a place located outside the city a bit. The Whistling Wind Motel. What do you think?"

"I'm sure it's fine." Curious, she asked, "Although, why is it important to be out of the city?"

"I'm just thinking it would be nice to stay in a place where there aren't a lot of other people." He flushed, adding, "Being in the city means there will be strangers around, those at the hotel or walking around outside. Keeping an eye on them will be nerve-racking and impossible to identify a bad guy until it's too late."

"Okay, the Whistling Wind it is," she agreed.

He made the call, asking for two connecting rooms. When he was finished, he put the SUV in gear and backed out of the parking spot. "Are you hungry? We could grab something to eat on the way."

"No, I'm fine. But if you're hungry, go ahead and stop."

"I have munchies in my bag," he admitted with a wry grin. "Chips, maybe a few cookies and some beef jerky, if you're interested."

"Ah, a junk food junkie?" She turned to face him. "I'm a vegan."

He almost choked. "You are? Really?"

She giggled. "No, but you should have seen your face. Hilarious."

He was glad she'd relaxed enough to joke around. Keeping a wary eye on the rearview mirror, he tried to make sure they weren't followed. But that was difficult to do while in the city with people coming and going.

According to the GPS on his dash, the motel was off one of the interstate exits. He turned and took the first ramp onto the freeway, knowing he'd feel better once they were out in the less populated area of town.

Traffic thinned on the interstate, which was a blessing. He stayed in the right lane, so that he could take the next exit to get to the motel.

As he got off the highway, he tapped the brake, but nothing happened. Tightening his grip on the steering wheel, he pressed down harder.

His foot went all the way to the floor.

What in the world? He pumped the brake, hoping and praying the vehicle would slow down, but it didn't.

Just the opposite. The SUV picked up speed as the exit ramp followed a downward incline. Panic gripped him by the throat. They were going to crash!

"Cash? What's wrong?"

"No brakes. Hang on!" He wrestled to keep the SUV under control, even as he sought for a way to bring the vehicle to a safe stop.

"Cash! A semitruck!"

"I see it!" The large eighteen-wheeler was heading across the road directly in front of them, going at a much slower speed. He didn't dare take his hands off the steering wheel, but Jacy reacted by leaning over and hitting the horn.

The truck lumbered on, as if the driver couldn't hear them.

Cash could tell the road up ahead was only one lane, with just a small shoulder off to the right. He struggled to keep the vehicle off to the side of the road, desperately praying they wouldn't hit the semitruck.

They didn't hit the semi, but the SUV continued careening forward, picking up even more speed. There was a large field off to the right, so Cash did the only thing he could think of to stop the speeding vehicle.

He wrenched the wheel, turning off the road and out onto the field. They'd barely made it five feet before the vehicle hit something, a rock or a tree stump, he wasn't sure. Instantly the SUV flew up and flipped over. The airbags deployed, sending a burst of pain through his face and head even as the SUV continued rolling over and over again, until it finally came to a stop against a small hill.

"Jacy!" He batted the airbag out of the way so he could turn to find Jacy. "Are you okay? Are you hurt?"

She groaned and lifted her head. He didn't see any blood, but that didn't mean anything. She could have internal injuries or worse.

"Wh-what happened?" She glanced around in confusion. "We crashed?"

"You don't remember?" His gut tightened with fear.

"No, I do, but…" She lifted a hand to her head. "I don't understand why we crashed."

He reached over to unlatch his seat belt and then helped her with hers. "I think someone tampered with the brake line, made a small hole in it. Can you move? We need to get out of here."

"Tampered with it?" Jacy stared at him for a long moment. "Like, on purpose? Who? The same person you chased outside my apartment building?"

"I believe so, yes." He hated having to push her. "Come on, Jacy. We need to get out of here."

"Okay." She shoved at her door, but it wouldn't open.

Cash managed to pry his door open enough that he could get out. Then he ran around to her side, but it was no use. That part of the vehicle was up against the hill's incline. He hurried back to the driver's-side door. "I'm sorry, but you're going to need to crawl out this way."

She grimaced and leaned forward. Somehow, she managed to lift herself up and over the center console, and finally out the door. He hauled her into his arms, holding her close for a long moment.

It was only through God's grace that they'd survived the crash. That and the safety features built into all cars these days. All five of the interior airbags had deployed. He and Jacy would be bruised, but they'd survive.

"Why? Why is this happening?"

"I don't know." He didn't want to let her go, but they couldn't stay here. "Lean against the car for a moment."

She did as he asked.

He reached in and pulled her bag out, then went around to the rear hatch. The window was broken, giving him enough room to reach inside to grab his overnight bag and his laptop. He hurried back to where Jacy was leaning against the SUV. "Can you walk? The hotel isn't far."

"Of course." She let out a soft moan as she pushed away from the vehicle.

He slipped his arm around her waist. "Lean on me."

As they made their way back across the field, he raked his gaze over the area, searching for the perp who'd done this.

There was no sign of anyone, but he knew the assailant was out there somewhere.

And that person had just tried to kill them.

THREE

Jacy's entire body ached, but she didn't complain. They were alive and that was all that mattered.

"We'll need to call a rideshare and get you checked out at the closest hospital," Cash said.

"I don't think that's necessary," she protested.

"I do." His tone held a note of finality.

"What about you?" She turned to look at his grim profile. "I'm not getting checked unless you do, too. We were both in the same crash."

He hesitated then grumbled, "Fine. We'll both get examined by a doc. For now, let's keep moving. It will be easier to get a rideshare at the motel, rather than having someone pick us up in the middle of a cornfield."

The uneven terrain made it difficult to walk, especially when her muscles were screaming in protest. They were sore, but she didn't think she had any broken bones. Thankfully, the airbags and seat belts had done their job.

"I can't believe the brake line was tampered with," she murmured.

"Hard to prove for sure, but the SUV is relatively new, so I'm going with the theory this was no accident."

"You were almost killed because of me." The realization sank deep into her bones.

"Not because of you. Because of the perp." He tightened his grip around her waist. "I thank God I was here with you, Jacy."

Her throat tensed with emotion. "Me, too."

They reached the Whistling Wind Motel ten minutes later. Rather than check into their rooms, Cash called for a rideshare. "We can't stay the night here, anyway," he confided in a low tone. "Too close to the crash scene."

The trip to the Emergency Department didn't take as long as she'd feared. Just telling them they'd been in a rollover crash was enough to get them into rooms right away. Cash must have made the call to Detective Vargas because he came in shortly after she'd been scanned from head to toe.

"I already heard what happened from Detective Rawson," Vargas said. "Do you have anything to add?"

"No. Other than I was afraid we were going to hit the semitruck at more than sixty-five miles per hour." She shivered at the memory. "I still can't figure out how Cash managed to avoid it."

"I understand these incidents may be related to a perp you helped put away," Vargas said. "Do you have any ideas on who that might be? Besides Felicia Gephardt?"

"Maybe someone hired by Jonah King." She exhaled a breath then added, "I'll make a list of all the names I can remember. Maybe going through my portfolio of sketches will help."

"That would be great." Vargas's expression softened. "I'm glad you and Rawson aren't hurt too badly."

"Me, too." Right after Vargas left, the doctor returned.

"No signs of internal bleeding, just bumps and bruises. I'll make sure you have a prescription for pain meds to take with you."

"No need." Jacy shook her head then winced at the soreness of her neck. "I'd rather stick with over-the-counter meds."

"Okay, you're free to go, then." The doctor turned and left just as Cash came in.

"Ah, Jacy. You should take the prescription," he advised. "Tomorrow you'll feel worse than today."

She swung her legs over to sit on the edge of the bed. "Did you take a prescription?"

"No," he reluctantly admitted.

"I didn't think so." She stood and took a deep breath before reaching for her coat. "Let's get out of here."

"I found another motel." Cash slung both their bags and his laptop over his shoulder. "We'll use a rideshare for now and work on getting a rental car tomorrow. I don't want to keep bugging Vargas for help unless we really need it."

She stifled a groan as she shrugged into her coat. "We could check in the morning to see if my car is ready. It's been in the shop for repairs."

"I'd rather get a rental. At least with a vehicle not related to either one of us, we should be safe."

She wanted to believe that, but couldn't seem to shake the lingering apprehension. Maybe if she could come up with a list of suspects, it would be easier to look at these attacks from a logical perspective.

Rather than from fear.

The rideshare driver took them to a chain motel that

was roughly seven miles from the hospital. Thankfully, Cash was able to get two adjoining rooms.

"Open the connecting door for me, okay?" He set her bag on her bed.

"Sure." After doing so, she sank down into the closest chair. Her muscles were already stiff and sore, and she didn't even want to imagine what tomorrow might bring.

Cash joined her a few minutes later. He took the seat across from her, the munchies from his bag scattered on the table. She reached for a potato chip. "I know we need to make a list of suspects for these recent incidents, but I also wanted to ask you what you remember from that night ten years ago."

She groaned. "Don't you think I've tried to probe those missing memories before now? Especially after Claire went missing? I don't remember anything new."

"Please, Jacy? For me?" He offered a crooked smile. "I know you were on your way home from choir practice."

"Yes. We had a small twelve-person choir that was set to compete at state."

"Have you joined a choir here in Appleton?"

"No." Jacy looked down at her lap, hardly able to remember her life before the attack. "I never sang again and my parents homeschooled me for the rest of my high school years, too. Although, after I was finished, they ended up getting divorced."

He winced. "I'm sorry to hear that. It sounds as if you enjoyed singing in the choir."

"I did." She shrugged. "After the attack, I became focused on art instead."

"I've seen your drawings. You're a very talented artist."

"My skill is more in extracting details from witnesses and managing to portray them on paper." She lifted her eyes to his and smiled. "I learned from a seasoned forensic artist who discovered this as her second career after she was a victim herself. She was incredible."

"I think you're incredible," he said.

She rolled her eyes. "Yeah, so incredible that I can't remember anything from the attack."

"You're doing your best, which is all I can ask." He paused then said, "You always took the same route home from school, correct?"

"Yes. I lived in an older neighborhood, while most of my friends lived in the new suburb." She smiled wryly. "You know, the one with the more expensive houses."

"Hey, I didn't live in the expensive neighborhood, either. Nothing stood out as unusual as you walked home?"

"No. I was thinking about our practice and humming under my breath as I went. As the soprano, I had to hit the high notes and I'd flubbed a few during the practice. Or so my choir teacher claimed." At the time, she'd been upset at the criticism, something that was so meaningless now.

"Interesting, those details weren't in the police report."

"They weren't?" She frowned. "I'm sure I mentioned it to Detective Jane Ash."

"I'm sure you did. Detective Ash retired from the Madison PD three years ago. I took this case over from her."

"I knew that's why you came to see me," she murmured.

"I can't lie to you, Jacy. Once I heard about the second missing girl, I knew I needed to talk to you again. Please don't be upset with me."

"I'm not." How could she be upset about a cop who wanted to put the bad guy behind bars, especially one who'd rushed to her rescue?

"What is the last house on the street that you can remember?"

She tilted her head, regarding him thoughtfully. "I remember going past the Colgate house. We called it that because of the white fence out front that badly needed a coat of paint. You know, like teeth needing to be cleaned with Colgate toothpaste."

"Do you remember who lived there?"

She wrinkled her nose. "Not really, they were an older couple. I didn't interact with them much."

"Okay, so you saw the Colgate house," he prodded. He took a bite of beef jerky. "Then what?"

"The next thing I remember is waking up to see your face leaning over me in the darkness. I saw you, then realized my entire body hurt, much the way it does now." She furrowed her brow, adding, "You told me I fell down the hill, landing at the bottom of the ravine."

"Yes, that's true. I was a witness back then, so it helps me to have you go through the details again. Do you remember anything else?"

"You were sweet and kind, telling me to stay down until the ambulance arrived. You covered me with your coat." Her eyes abruptly widened. "I didn't have my coat. The attacker must have kept it!"

"Yes, you were not wearing a coat that night. It's one of the things I noticed, considering the temperature was only ten degrees outside. That and the way you were running, as if you had no idea where you were going."

She frowned. "What makes you say that?"

"You ran right across the road without looking, slipping on small patches of snow." He waved a hand. "There was a less icy route you could have taken, but didn't. I had the impression you were running in blind panic. It was the main reason, along with the fact that you were not wearing a coat, that I followed you."

"A blind panic," she repeated softly. "I don't remember running or falling."

"You don't remember anything between seeing the Colgate house and seeing me looking down at you."

"That's correct." A wave of annoyance hit hard. "Look, I get you're trying to uncover the truth. But I don't remember. I desperately wish I did. Those girls…" Her voice trailed off.

"The fact that they went missing isn't your fault," he quickly interjected. "We don't even know if there's a connection between what happened ten years ago and the two recent cases at all."

"But you drove up from Madison because you think there is a possible link."

"I do, yes. And to see if you'd be willing to walk with me through the crime scene, the ravine where I found you." He shrugged. "We can also walk around the high school grounds to see if something sparks your memory. Although, you should know my boss thinks I'm way off base."

She stared at him for a long moment. "I don't know if it's better or worse to have these cases connected. Ten years, Cash. Well, nine considering three other girls disappeared after the attack on me over the course of several months. But why would an assailant kidnap me, and three others, then disappear for that length of time only to reemerge now?"

"I know, it's not logical." He paused for a long moment then pulled several photographs from his pocket and began setting them out on the table.

Five different teenage faces stared up at her. Claire, Suzanna, along with the other three girls who had disappeared in Madison after Jacy's attack—Emily, Beth, Kim—and Jacy.

She stared at them for several long moments. Seeing their young faces made her feel sick with dread, the chips congealing in her stomach. What had happened to them?

"We all look similar." Her voice was agonizingly soft. "Young, long blond hair..."

"This is why I had to take the chance to question you again, Jacy." He quickly gathered the photographs together and stuffed them back into his pocket. "Not to make you relive the worst night of your life, but to see if there was anything that might remotely help find the man who did this."

"If they're dead, it's my fault." She shivered, wondering who could be so cruel and callous. "My fault, because there's nothing but a black hole in my memory where the assailant's face should be."

"It's not your fault," he protested. But she wasn't listening.

Five young girls were missing or dead. And Cash thought she was the only one who could help find them.

Cash watched as Jacy pushed herself up, stumbling away from the small table. "Jacy, don't, please." He lunged toward her.

She roughly shook off his hand. "I need a minute." Without waiting for his response, she disappeared into the bathroom.

Cash wished there was more he could do to help Jacy regain her memory of the attack. Other than asking her to walk the crime scene again back in Madison, he couldn't think of anything else he could do to find these missing girls.

When Jacy didn't come out of the bathroom right away, he crossed over to the door. "Jacy? Are you okay?"

"Fine. Just tired."

"Get some sleep, we'll talk more in the morning." He wanted to pull her into his arms but forced himself to leave her alone.

She'd been through a lot over the past few hours. He should have waited until morning to question her. He finished up the beef jerky and packed the snacks away. He needed to rest.

The following morning, he woke early, despite his fitful sleep. When he heard Jacy moving around in her room, he lightly rapped on the door. "Would you like coffee? And breakfast? I ordered from room service."

"Yes, please."

He made the small pot of coffee provided by the hotel. Jacy joined him, looking better than she had the night before. A knock at the door indicated their food had arrived, and he gave the young server a tip before bringing the tray into the room.

He set it on the table then glanced at her. "I'm sorry. I hope you're not upset with me for asking questions last night."

"No, of course not." She held up a piece of paper.

"I began my list of suspects that match my sketches. I still have more to go through, but thought Detective Vargas could work on checking them out while we head to Madison."

"I'd like to do that, too." He was impressed she'd gotten so many names written down and that she'd readily agreed to return to Madison. "You're amazing, Jacy. Thanks."

"You're welcome." She took a sip of her coffee and joined him at the small table. "Smells delicious."

"I'd like to say grace." He cleared his throat. "Dear Lord, we thank You for keeping us safe in Your care. Amen."

"Amen," she murmured.

"Dig in," he teased, pointing his fork at her strawberry topped waffles then diving into his omelet.

They ate in silence for a few minutes. "Cash, why isn't the FBI involved in the missing girls' case?"

"They are. I've spoken to Special Agent Kyle Boyd, and he is willing to provide additional assistance to us." He shrugged. "Unfortunately, we don't have many leads to follow up on. According to Vargas, no witnesses have come forward on the two most recent cases."

"There's still time." She frowned. "Suzanna only disappeared twenty-four hours ago."

"I know. I'm hopeful something will break soon on these recent cases here in Appleton." He sighed. "If we find the person responsible, we may be able to link him to the cases from ten years ago, too. Including yours, Jacy."

"Yeah, maybe."

"I work the cases of the missing girls who disappeared after your attack every chance I get. I don't want them to be forgotten."

"I admire your dedication." Her green gaze clung to his.

"It's my job." He shifted in his seat and continued eating. Jacy had moved away from Madison, and he knew full well she would not be interested in maintaining a relationship with a man who reminded her of the attack she'd narrowly escaped.

And he wasn't ready to try a relationship again, either. He found it easier to stay focused on his cases if he didn't have to worry about someone else. Lana, his former fiancée, had gotten tired of his late hours and tough cases. Looking back, he couldn't blame her.

And if he were completely honest, he didn't miss her complaining, either.

"You're still planning to get a rental car?" Jacy asked. "We could see if my car is finished at the garage."

"I'd rather use a rental. And I'd like to drop off your list with Vargas first. We can both work the names, while you try to come up with additional ones."

"Sounds good, but we're going to Madison, right?" She eyed him over the rim of her cup.

He hesitated, nodded. "As I said, I was hoping you'd be willing to retrace your steps that night. If you're up to it, Jacy. If not, that's okay."

"I'll do it, Cash, because these missing girls need to be found." She sounded as if she were trying to convince herself more so than him. "This is the least I can do."

"Thank you." He reached over to touch her hand. "You're a strong, brave woman, Jacy."

"I'm not." She winced. "I tried hypnosis once, ten years ago, but it didn't work. Apparently, I'm immune."

"Really?" He was surprised to hear it. "Okay, we could consider trying again later." He glanced at his watch. "For now, I need to get another rideshare."

As the rideshare driver took them back to the precinct, which was beginning to feel like a home away from home, he thought about her failed attempt at hypnosis.

Were some people really immune to hypnosis? Or was this a case of Jacy refusing to allow herself to relax enough to open her mind to it?

Probably not the time to ask.

Ten minutes later, their driver let them off at the precinct. It was still early, so he figured there wouldn't be any new information. At least they could leave Jacy's list with Vargas.

When he and Jacy went inside, Vargas immediately came out to meet them. "Hey, I was just going to call you."

His pulse kicked up a notch. "You have Gephardt? Is she talking?"

"No, unfortunately we haven't found her." Vargas looked disgruntled. "She hasn't been home. I got permission to have a squad car parked outside her apartment building all night. We swung by the restaurant where she works and found the manager was already on site. She informed us that Felicia called off sick today."

Cash blew out a long breath. "Not helpful."

"No," Vargas agreed, shooting an apologetic glance at Jacy. "I'm sorry about this. I told the manager to call me if she shows up or if she calls again. I also have Gephardt's cell number, which I've called twice without a response. I'm hoping to hear from her or maybe her lawyer soon." Vargas paused before adding, "I've started looking into King's known associates, but I haven't found anything. He's allegedly been a model prison inmate. If he's holding a grudge, he's hiding it well."

"Thanks for the update." Cash knew the detective was doing his best.

"Here are more possible suspects." Jacy handed over the list of names, which Cash had taken a picture of with his phone. "I'll keep working on adding to the list, but thought it was a place to start."

"Thanks." Vargas eyeballed it. "This is great. I'll call you if we learn anything new."

"Okay. We're heading to Madison for a while," Cash informed the detective. "I was wondering if you could give us a lift to the airport so I can rent a car since ours is toast."

"Why Madison?" Vargas asked. "I have a vehicle here you can use for the next few days. It's one that we use for undercover operations."

"That would be great." Cash glanced at Jacy, wondering how much she wanted the detective to know. "I'm following up a lead in Madison and Jacy is coming along for the ride."

"Okay." Vargas arched a brow as if sensing there was more. "It's good you'll be out of town, Jacy. I'm sure the assailant behind these attacks will never find you in Madison."

"Exactly," Cash agreed. "But please don't hesitate to call if you learn something. It would be very helpful to know if Gephardt or King are involved in these attacks."

"Yeah. Hang on, I'll get you a set of keys." Vargas turned away, returning a few minutes later. "This is a four-wheel-drive Jeep, parked out back. Drive safe. We might be getting snow later today."

"We will, thanks a lot." He shouldered their overnight bags and his laptop to head outside. Finding the Jeep was no problem, and soon they were back on the road.

"Does Vargas or any of the other cops you work with know about your attack from ten years ago?"

"I haven't talked about it, but if they did any research on me, I'm sure they found the news articles about it." She shrugged. "They probably know more than I realize."

"How many precincts do you work for?"

"A dozen spread across a hundred miles or so." She sent him a sidelong glance. "I like my job and the variety of cases I'm involved with. I've even worked with a few Amish witnesses. They did remarkably well in providing details for me to work with."

"That's interesting, I didn't think the Amish worked with law enforcement."

"They often don't, but Liam—er, Sheriff Harland, has a good rapport with the Green Lake Amish community."

He was impressed with her decision to work in law enforcement, her way of giving back to the community.

He brought up the GPS on the screen to find the quickest route to Madison. "Ready?"

"Of course." She put on a brave face. He was glad to note her eyes were no longer red and puffy from the chemicals. She was beautiful as always, although the moment that thought entered his brain, he ruthlessly shoved it out.

"If traffic is light," he said as he left the parking lot, "we should be able to make it to Madison in two hours."

"Sounds good." Her tone lacked enthusiasm.

"Jacy, if you don't want to do this, I'll understand." He reached over to take her hand. "No hard feelings."

"I'll do it." She sounded stronger now. "I hate thinking about those missing girls."

"Me, too." He forced himself to release her hand to turn his attention to the road. The GPS had the exit toward Madison as less than ten minutes away.

As he picked up speed, a loud popping sound rang out, followed by the shrill of shattering glass as the rear passenger window exploded.

Cold air whipped around them as he fought to keep the Jeep on the road. Then suddenly, the interior of the vehicle began to fill with thick dark smoke. It burned his eyes and made it impossible to see the road.

What was going on? Tightening his grip on the steering wheel, he slowed and tried to pull over onto the side of the road, hoping and praying they didn't crash.

The Jeep came to a jarring halt, their front end jammed into the concrete barrier. Straining to see through his burning eyes, he turned toward Jacy. Before he could say anything, she cried out in alarm.

"No! Stop! Cash! Help me!"

"Jacy!" He tried to find and hold on to her, praying he was strong enough to prevent the assailant from taking her away.

FOUR

"I've got you again, Jacy." The voice was a low whisper, sounding exactly like the assailant at her apartment. She felt the seat belt give way and realized with horror that the perp outside the vehicle had sliced it with a knife.

"No. Let me go!" Jacy jerked back from the tight grip on her arm with all the strength she could muster. "Cash, help me. He's trying to kidnap me!"

"Let her go!" Thankfully, Cash's strong arms slid beneath her arm pits, hauling her up and over the center console, away from the door. Since the seat belt wasn't holding her in place, she was able to kick out with her feet, hitting something solid. A muffled grunt gave her a surge of satisfaction.

She kicked again and again, striking the person she couldn't see, until the hand abruptly fell away from her arm. The sound of police sirens filled the air and when she kicked through the open door again, her foot found nothing but air.

"He's gone," she gasped. The smoke burned her eyes, much like the pepper spray had. Was it possible this assailant was trying to blind her permanently? The

gruesome thought made her feel sick to her stomach.
"Cash, please. We need to get out of here."

Fresh air wafted through her open passenger door,
helping to dissipate the smoke that hung heavily inside the Jeep. She blinked and stared outside, hoping
to get a glimpse of the assailant. A figure in dark clothing darted across the road, toward a nearby vehicle.
A truck?

"No! He's getting away!" She struggled against
Cash's embrace, intent on getting out of their borrowed
wrecked vehicle to get a license plate number. Cash let
her go, and she scrambled from the Jeep, wiping at her
eyes to clear the stinging smoke from them.

But it was too late.

The dark vehicle was gone.

Jacy's shoulders slumped as she sank back against
the side of the damaged Jeep. Cars whizzed past them
as Cash joined her.

"Do you know for sure it was the same assailant?"
Cash asked. His red-rimmed eyes must have mirrored
her own. The smoke bomb had done its job, blinding
them both to the point she was nearly kidnapped again.

"It was the same person as outside my apartment,
saying, 'I've got you again, Jacy.'" She reached up to
brush her hair from her face. "I'm sure he used the
smoke bomb on purpose to blind us, the same way he
used pepper spray." She swallowed hard and added,
"I'm getting the sense this is a guy, not a woman. But
I wish I could say for sure."

"He tried to pull you out of the car." Cash's voice
was hoarse.

"Yes, but he hadn't anticipated the seat belt." She
shook her head. "Not a smart move because he had to

cut the seat belt to get me out of the Jeep. And when you helped haul me backward over the center console and away from him and the door, I was able to kick him." She sighed. "Between the kicks to the gut and the police sirens, he let me go."

"It's interesting that he keeps using smoke or other substances to keep you from seeing him clearly." Cash put his arm around her waist and drew her farther from the vehicle as a squad car approached. "That tells me he thinks you can identify him."

"Or he's using that as a mechanism to prevent me from drawing his features." She shivered, not from the chilly January air but because this attacker was succeeding in his mission.

She couldn't draw him, no matter how much she wanted to have him arrested.

"I need my eyesight to work, Cash," she whispered. "It's almost as if he's determined to prevent me from drawing any police sketches ever again."

"I don't know what to say. Except to be thankful God has watched over us again."

"Yeah." She wasn't sure what to think. Cash was a believer, which was nice. When she'd done those sketches for Sheriff Liam Harland, she'd discovered he'd been a religious man, too. She thought it was from his association with the Amish.

But that wouldn't explain Cash's faith.

She didn't know many men who were believers, but found herself glad to be with Cash. Before she could say anything more, an officer from the police vehicle came over to talk to them. Her eyes burned, but she was able to make out his last name was Papp.

"What happened? Did you lose control of the vehicle?" Officer Papp's brow creased as he reached for a notebook, seemingly prepared to write Cash a ticket.

"No, Officer. I'm Detective Cash Rawson, and I've been working with Detective Dennis Vargas." Cash flashed his badge, which seemed to surprise Officer Papp. "This was no accident. If you look inside, you'll find the remnants of a smoke bomb that was fired into the vehicle through the back window. I'm not sure if the perp used a shot gun or some other type of weapon. All I know is that we were blinded from the smoke billowing up inside the vehicle."

Officer Papp peered through the window of the Jeep then whistled under his breath. "This is a new one for me. I've never seen anything like this."

His comment would have made her smile under different circumstances. Unfortunately, there was nothing humorous in the escalating attempt against them.

She stepped forward, imploring him with her gaze. "Please call Detective Vargas for us, Officer Papp. The detective needs to be aware of this attack. Oh, and he was the one who loaned the Jeep to us in the first place. It's not even our vehicle. It belongs to the Appleton Police Department."

"Really?" The officer's eyes rounded with amazement. "Yeah, okay. Give me a few minutes to touch base with Vargas." Officer Papp turned away to speak into the radio clipped to his collar.

Cash opened the back passenger door of the Jeep and pulled their bags out, slinging them over his shoulder. The two duffels and the laptop were soon out of the vehicle. "We're going to need a ride to the airport to get that rental after all," he muttered.

"What I don't understand is how the assailant knew

we were in the Jeep." She frowned, glancing around the busy interstate. "It couldn't be that he just happened to notice us in time to toss a smoke bomb into the car."

"No, you're right about that. Whoever this guy is, he must have been watching the police precinct, assuming we'd show up after the crash the night before." Cash scowled. "Or there's a leak inside the Appleton Police Department."

"No way, I don't believe that. Detective Vargas is a good guy," she protested.

"Not Vargas, but anyone else there could have discovered he'd loaned us the Jeep. Even the guy behind the desk saw him leave and return with the keys, telling us exactly where the Jeep was located." Cash sounded seriously annoyed. He slammed the door with more force than was necessary. "From this point forward, we're not telling anyone anything."

"That's fine with me," she agreed.

Officer Papp returned with a sheepish expression in his eyes. "Vargas filled me in on what the two of you have been dealing with. I'm sorry to hear you've come under attack yet again. Vargas gave me instructions to give you a ride back to the precinct. I know he wants both of you to provide statements on what transpired here."

"No, we're not going back," Cash said firmly. "We'll give Vargas our statement over the phone. What we really need is a ride to the airport."

"I—uh, okay." Officer Papp looked surprised but then gestured toward his vehicle. "I'll take you wherever you'd like to go. You'd better call Detective Vargas on the way. He sounded like he really wants to talk to you."

Cash grunted in what she took for agreement while opening the door of the squad car for her. She quickly climbed inside, hoping they'd be safe inside a police vehicle.

Once they were seated, Cash made the call to Detective Vargas. She listened as he gave a brief overview of what had happened, not surprised when he then handed the phone to her.

"Jacy? What in the world happened? Are you sure this is the same guy?"

"Yes, I'm positive this was the same person who assaulted me with pepper spray outside my apartment." She met Officer Papp's glance in the rearview mirror; he was listening intently to their conversation. No doubt he'd have to include some of this in his own report to his boss. "The guy spoke in the same hushed whisper, called me by name and tried to pull me from the car just like he tried to pull me from my apartment building last night. The difference this time was that he had to cut through the seat belt holding me in place. Thankfully, at that moment, Cash pulled me back toward him, and I was able to kick the assailant several times in the belly, which forced him to let me go."

"Did you recognize the voice?" Vargas asked. "Can you narrow down if it's male or female?"

"I wish I could." It was beyond frustrating that every time this guy came at her, he blinded her. "All I can say with certainty is that it was the same voice as the person who attacked me at my apartment." She hesitated before continuing. "I still have no idea who is coming after me or why." Well, the why part had to be linked to her police work, but the assailant's identity was still a mystery.

"I don't like that you were found in our Jeep," Vargas said. "To be honest, I think your plan to rent is a good one."

She glanced at Cash, who still looked grim. Had he told Vargas their plan to rent a car, or had the detective assumed that was the plan based on the Jeep getting wrecked? "Yeah, thanks."

Cash held out his hand for the phone, so she gave it back. "Listen, Vargas, nothing personal but we're going to stay off-grid for a while. I would rather not have any ties to you or anyone else at the precinct." Cash listened for a moment then said, "Yes, I will find a way to get in touch with you at some point for an update on the case. But in the meantime, I don't want anyone to know where we are or what we're driving, understand?"

There was another long pause as Vargas said something in response.

"All I will commit to is that you'll hear from us when we have time. That will have to be good enough for now." Another pause then, "Thanks, Detective. Take care." With that, Cash disconnected from the call. He shocked her by opening his window and tossing his phone out. He turned to her and wiggled his fingers, indicating he wanted her phone, too.

"But my work…" The protest was automatic, yet it didn't take but another few seconds to realize how foolish it was to argue. At the rate this assailant was coming after them, she wouldn't survive long enough to have a job. Not if they couldn't figure out who this guy was. She pulled her phone from her pocket and handed it over. That one went out the window as well.

It was a strange feeling to be completely disconnected from the outside world. No phone, no way to keep in touch with anyone. No job, at least in the interim.

And no place to call home.

She swallowed hard, battling a wave of panic. She wasn't afraid of Cash; he'd done nothing but support her and keep her safe since showing up in the nick of time to prevent the pepper spray assailant from kidnapping her. But that was a long way from knowing anything about him personally.

Had he ever been married, divorced? Have kids? He'd popped back into her life at the right time to rescue her, but now they were pretty much stuck with each other.

Their lives depended on their ability to figure out who was coming after her and how, if at all, the attacks were related to the missing girls.

A seemingly insurmountable task.

Jacy remained quiet as Officer Papp navigated the traffic. When they arrived at the small airport, Cash was relieved. He was anxious to move on with their badly needed anonymity.

"Thanks, Officer." He nodded when Papp let them out of the back of the car.

"Anytime." Papp's eyebrows were furrowed with concern. "Stay safe."

"Yeah, that's the plan." Cash stood beside Jacy, their bags slung over his shoulder, waiting until Officer Papp drove away before turning to search for the rental car sign. "This way," he said, nodding toward the closest rental counter.

Jacy fell into step beside him, still unusually quiet. Maybe tossing their phones out the window had been a bit drastic, but they'd been under siege for less than twenty-four hours. And that was more than enough.

The entire situation was getting out of hand. At this point, he didn't want anything to tie them back to the Appleton PD or to Jacy's apartment.

It didn't take him long to secure another SUV. Jacy still hadn't said anything when he stored their bags and his laptop in the back of the vehicle.

"Are you okay?" He raked his eyes over her, wondering if he'd missed an injury of some sort. "We didn't hit the side of the barrier that hard."

"How can I be okay?" Her voice sounded harsh. "I'm stranded with you for the foreseeable future! I don't know who keeps coming after me or why, and I don't know anything about you other than you're a cop."

"Whoa, Jacy, you know me." He reached out to touch her arm, but she jerked away. "I'm the same guy who found you ten years ago at the bottom of the ravine."

"Ten years, Cash." She huffed out a sigh then asked, "Do you have a girlfriend? Wife? Fiancée? Kids?"

"None of the above, although I was seeing someone up until a year or so ago. We were engaged to be married." It was a little cold to be standing in the parking garage talking, but Jacy obviously needed some reassurance. "Until Lana decided she didn't want to be with a cop anymore and left me."

She looked at him for a long moment. "I'm sorry to hear that."

He shrugged. "Don't be. I don't think I loved her as much as I should have, since I didn't miss having her around as much as I thought I would."

"Yet you asked her to marry you."

He shuffled his feet, feeling his cheeks warm with

embarrassment. "Well, technically, she asked me. We ended up shopping for a ring together, as Lana had very specific ideas on what sort of ring she wanted."

"I see." Jacy tipped her head to the side. "I bet she kept the ring, too, didn't she?"

"Yes, but what was I going to do with it?" He waved a hand. "That's not important. I want you to be comfortable with me. To know that I would never, ever hurt you."

"I do know that." She blew out a sigh. "I'm sorry, it sounds idiotic, but losing my phone has made me feel— isolated and vulnerable. Which is ridiculous, because it's just a phone."

"Your feelings are important." He eased a step closer, wishing he could pull her into his arms. "I care about you, Jacy. I'm sorry that going off-grid is scary. It's just that we keep getting found and we need time to get to the bottom of what's going on here."

"I know." She offered a crooked smile. "I apologize for going off the deep end."

He reached again for her hand and this time she didn't pull away. "We're going to be okay, Jacy. I promise to do everything humanly possible to protect you."

She tightened her grip on his hand and stepped closer. "I know you will. Thank you."

He put his arm around her shoulders and gave her a brief hug, keeping the embrace light and nonthreatening. "You didn't mention a boyfriend, fiancé or husband, either."

She arched a brow then nodded. "Okay, that's fair. I dated a guy for a while. A cop, actually, but he cheated on me. I can't say I've bothered to try the dating scene again."

Her comment about the cheater being a cop stung a bit. He wanted to point out that not all cops were cheaters, but that would sound as if he were vying for the chance to date her. That was ludicrous. Jacy wouldn't be interested in a guy who held memories of her past she'd rather forget.

And he didn't blame her.

"I'm sorry to hear things didn't end well, but I appreciate you letting me know." He privately thought the guy was a jerk to cheat on a woman like Jacy. "If you're okay, let's hit the road." He glanced around, glad that none of the rental car employees were paying them any attention. "Maybe this time, we can get to Madison without a car malfunction or being hit by a smoke bomb."

"Yeah, let's hope so." She didn't sound too confident.

"I'll take an alternate route." He didn't have his phone to use, but the rental car was relatively new and would have a GPS built in. "We'll avoid the interstate and take rural highways. It will add time to the trip, but I'm hoping this is better for us in the long run."

"Okay." She pulled away to open the passenger's-side door. "Do you think this attacker knows we were planning to head to Madison?"

He hesitated, unwilling to lie. "He might know that's our ultimate destination, but he won't be able to follow us there."

She nodded and ducked into the passenger seat. He quickly slid in behind the wheel, too, anxious to get out of Appleton.

Yet her question about the assailant knowing their ultimate destination nagged at him. So far, all the attacks against Jacy had taken place around Appleton, not Madison.

The most recent missing girls were also from Appleton. But if these vicious attacks were somehow related to Jacy's attack ten years ago, they would be heading right back into the hornet's nest.

Doubt assailed him. Should he just head to a different city? Maybe Green Bay? Somewhere no one would think to look for them?

Running away wasn't his style, but he had Jacy's well-being to consider as well. As he left the Appleton airport, he almost turned toward Green Bay, but forced himself to head in the opposite direction instead.

Two young high school girls were missing, and who knew how many others were at risk. No matter what they'd been through, Cash couldn't just ignore them.

No, he'd just have to find a way to make sure Jacy remained safe while they continued investigating the current attacks and the one that had taken place ten years ago.

In his gut, he knew the attack against Jacy was the one that had started the ball rolling. He wasn't sure why there'd been a nine-year gap in the assaults, other than the most obvious theory that the guy had been in jail. It didn't matter why; he remained convinced both Claire Simmons and Suzanna Perry were both taken by the same man.

An assailant Jacy couldn't remember.

FIVE

Staring with red-rimmed eyes out the passenger's-side window, Jacy struggled to hold herself together. Whoever this guy was, he seemed determined to get to her. What she didn't understand was why. Why her? Just because she'd sketched criminals to assist in finding and arresting them?

It was all so surreal. As if she might wake up from this to discover it was just a nightmare.

She drew in a deep cleansing breath, trying to relax. The assailant might know they were heading to Madison, but there's no way he could know what vehicle they were driving. The knowledge should have made her feel safe.

So not.

She watched as Cash navigated the traffic, weaving between cars as if trying to avoid anyone following them, until he exited the interstate. The GPS in the SUV provided an alternate route to Madison, which would take them two and a half hours. Using the back roads added another thirty minutes to their commute.

She still felt vulnerable without a phone. Glancing

at Cash, she said, "If we get in an accident, we won't be able to call for help."

"I know." He shrugged. "I plan to stop and pick up some disposable phones, but I'd like to push through to Madison, to get them there."

"Makes sense." She told herself a disposable phone was better than nothing. "I wish I could have left a message on my voice mail about being out of touch. I'm worried the various police precincts won't be able to get the help they need."

"I understand your concern, but there's nothing I can do about it." He arched a brow. "Have you ever taken a vacation?"

"Not really." She grimaced. "I've taken a few weekends off here and there, but my schedule is rather erratic anyway, so it seems silly to send a group email announcing I'm taking a few days off when I may not get a call in the first place."

"Okay, when we get to the motel, you can use my laptop to send an email. At least then the precincts you work with will know that you're not ignoring them."

"That works." Email wasn't as good as having a phone, but at least she wouldn't be leaving the cops among the various departments she worked with in limbo, waiting for her to respond.

If not for the missing girls, she wouldn't be sitting here beside Cash at all, heading back to the city where she'd been attacked long ago.

For years, she'd believed it was a blessing that she couldn't remember anything about the attack. One of her counselors had suggested her mind was protecting her from something horrible in blocking the memories.

Yet here she was, heading back to the city to pry the

locked box of memories open. She shivered but tried to ignore the deep sense of foreboding.

If unlocking the past was the key to saving lives, then she absolutely needed to try.

"Are you having second thoughts about this?"

Cash's question was far too close to the truth. "Rest assured, I'm determined to do this." She hesitated before saying, "I just can't guarantee this attempt to break through the wall surrounding my brain will work. I want to help find Claire and Suzanna. But it's been a long time since I tried to go back to the night I was attacked."

"Near the Colgate house," Cash said.

"I guess so, since it's the last place I remember." She frowned. "Did Detective Ash talk to the elderly couple who owned the place?"

"I believe everyone who lived on the route you took home that night was interviewed, yes." He met her gaze. "I plan to talk to them again, though. If they're still around and able to chat."

"I'm not sure going back all these years later to talk to them will help," she protested. "They were an elderly couple ten years ago. I highly doubt their memory has improved over time."

"You thought they were elderly at sixteen," Cash pointed out. "Chances are, they weren't as old as you assumed and are still around. Besides, the only way to know if they remember anything new is to ask."

"Maybe." She shifted in her seat, trying to ignore her aching muscles. The doc had been right about the next day being worse. She wouldn't have minded stopping at a drug store to get some ibuprofen. Something they could do when they picked up the disposable phones.

Thankfully, traffic wasn't an issue on the winding country highway. The curvy roads made it impossible to go very fast, but at least it was easy to see there was no one behind them.

Jacy wished she'd thought to grab her sketchbook and portfolio from her overnight bag stored in the back of the SUV. Closing her eyes, she mentally reviewed the sketches she'd done over the years, trying to add to the list she'd given Vargas.

She must have dozed a bit, because the next thing she knew the white dome of the Wisconsin Capitol building could be seen in the distance.

"Sorry about that." She flushed. "I didn't mean to sleep."

"I'm glad you were able to get some rest," Cash assured her. He gestured to the Capitol. "Does seeing that bring back any memories?"

"Not really, we didn't get downtown much when I was a kid." She hoped he wasn't going to ask her that with every landmark they passed. "I will say the traffic is more congested than I expected."

"Yeah, the growth in the city over the years has caused a lot of traffic nightmares," Cash agreed. "The original design of the city has become a problem. With the lakes on either side of the capital, there's only one road leading downtown."

She shook her head. "Just another reason I'm glad I don't live here anymore."

Cash didn't say anything for a long moment, making her realize she'd dismissed the place he'd chosen to call home.

"I'm sure it's a great place to work as a detective," she quickly added. "It's just not for me."

"I understand." He offered a wan smile. "I thought I'd drive through the neighborhood where you grew up, first, if that's okay?"

She tensed but nodded. "Sure, why not? May as well jump right in."

He shot her a questioning glance. "There's still time to change your mind."

"No, we need to do this."

He took the beltway around the city, heading to the neighborhood where she'd grown up. Where he'd grown up, too, she assumed, since he'd been on the road that night when she'd run away from her attacker.

She turned in her seat to face him. "Did you go to Woodridge High, too?"

"Yeah, I was three years ahead of you." He smiled. "Sorry to say, I don't remember you at all."

"What senior pays attention to a sophomore?" She wasn't surprised. "Odd to know that we went to the same school, though. I'm not sure why that realization hadn't occurred to me before now."

"You think your attacker is from Woodridge High?"

She spread her hands wide. "I don't remember, Cash. I wish I did. All I can say is anything is possible."

"Maybe we need to get a hold of some old high school yearbooks," he mused. "Maybe looking back will jar something loose."

"We can try." She peered through the window as he took the exit that would lead to their neighborhood. "It looks very different from what I remember."

"Youth has a way of distorting the past," Cash agreed. "This is one of the main reasons I wanted to bring you back here."

She wasn't sure how to respond to that. When he

pulled into the parking lot of the high school, she wanted to protest.

But, of course, this was why she'd come. To walk the path she'd taken that fateful night ten years ago.

When he stopped the SUV, she drew in a bracing breath before pushing out of the vehicle. She stood for a moment to reorient herself. She hadn't been back here since the attack, preferring to be homeschooled by her parents. The entire school looked smaller, but the auditorium where they'd held their choir practice that night was still visible on the north side of the building.

"I left through the side door there." She gestured to the exit.

Cash reached out to take her hand. "Let's go."

Being afraid to approach the school wasn't logical. It wasn't the location of her attack; she clearly remembered walking past the Colgate house. Pushing aside the lingering fear wasn't easy, but she did her best.

Fear would only prevent the memories from returning. She forced herself to picture Claire Simmons and Suzanna Perry. Two sixteen-year-old girls who needed to be found as soon as humanly possible.

She could and would do this. No matter the cost to her peace of mind.

"God is guiding you," Cash said in a low voice. "Trust in Him."

"I will." She squared her shoulders and picked up her pace. The sooner she completed this task, the better.

Cash hated having to force Jacy to relive the night of her attack, but he didn't see an alternative. He needed something, anything, to go on. Even the smallest and seemingly insignificant clue might help to find the missing girls.

"We may need to come back at night." Jacy's expression was thoughtful as she stood in front of the auditorium exit. The way she gripped his hand made him realize she appreciated having him close by. "It looks different in the daytime."

"We can try that, if you think it will help." He was surprised she'd suggested it. He'd wanted to jog her memory without dragging fear along for the ride. "Which way did you go from here?"

"Straight across the parking lot." She headed that way, tugging him along.

He let her take the lead, keeping pace easily enough. She had to take a few detours around parked cars, but they soon reached the opposite side of the school parking lot. She crossed the road and took another few steps to reach the sidewalk on the other side of the street.

"I said goodbye to a few kids from my choir group here." She stopped and turned to look around. "These houses look different for some reason. But I know this is where we parted ways. Some kids had cars, but those who walked lived in my neighborhood or in the more expensive subdivision located that way." She gestured to the west. "They were all alibied by their parents, so I know they weren't involved."

"Were you afraid to walk home alone?" he asked.

"Not then." She shrugged. "To be fair, I only live five blocks down from the school. And it wasn't that late, only about seven thirty at night. Dark in January, though."

"I have to admit, this has always been considered a safe neighborhood."

"Until it wasn't," she muttered. "Let's keep walking."

Once again, he let her take the lead. They walked a few blocks until she abruptly stopped. "Where's the Colgate house?"

His heart sank. "It's right there."

Jacy frowned. "Oh, I see, someone took the fence down. And they must have painted the house, too, because it wasn't blue. It was a dirty white color that pretty much matched the dirty white fence that used to encircle the front yard."

"Yes, it appears the house may have new owners." There was a small play area, indicating little kids spent some time here. Could be grandkids, but he had a feeling the original owners of the Colgate house, as Jacy referred to it, had moved on.

He chided himself for not interviewing them before now. Yet he couldn't deny feeling as if Jacy was the key to uncovering the truth. He'd see if he could find the former property owners, but watched Jacy as she stood on the sidewalk, looking around with confusion.

"I don't know, Cash. This all looks different to me."

"Take your time," he urged. "Imagine the fence is still there. Can you tell me where you were standing when you last remember being here?"

She took two steps forward. "Here, I think. I remember being just past the front door."

"What caused you to stop here?" Cash asked.

"I—I'm not sure." She grimaced and turned in a circle. "My house was up on the next block. Maybe I heard something? Or saw something?"

He masked his disappointment, knowing she was

doing the best she could. "Okay, let's keep walking a bit."

"Why? I know I didn't get all the way home. I'm sure I'd have remembered that."

"I know, but we've come this far. May as well go a little further."

She reached out to take his hand. He longed to pull her close, but reminded himself she was only looking for emotional support, nothing more.

They were silent as they walked down the next block. This time, Jacy recognized the house where she'd grown up. "It looks the same, yet smaller."

"Perceptions about size are often distorted by youth." He gave her hand a small squeeze. "If you would walk back into the high school, the entire building would seem smaller, too. At least, it did for me."

She nodded, her gaze lingering on the house. "I haven't lived here in a long time, but it seems longer. Like decades."

He gave it another minute before turning to head back toward the school, where he'd left the rental. "Let's stop at a store to get the disposable phones, then find a place to stay."

"And get lunch?" Jacy asked.

"We may start with that," he agreed with a soft chuckle. "I'm hungry."

She glanced over her shoulder one last time. "I hope the family living there now is happy."

He frowned. "You weren't happy living there?"

"I was, until that night. My life changed dramatically after that. Between the nightmares and the irrational fears I carried around, I didn't leave the house for several months after the attack." She shrugged. "My parents started to argue about me, too. It wasn't until I stumbled across an article about forensic sketching that something clicked in my mind. I'd taken up sketching, but in that moment I knew I needed to pursue this as a career. Having a goal helped me push past my fears to apply for the program. Thankfully, I was accepted. I studied in Chicago then moved to Appleton."

"I hope you know how amazing you are," he said in a low voice. "It must have been difficult for you to conquer your fears, but you did it. And thanks to you, the police have been able to put many bad guys behind bars."

"Bad guys and women," she corrected wryly. "Like Felicity Gephardt."

"Once we have replacement phones, we'll follow up with Vargas. Hopefully, they have her in custody by now."

"That would be good to know, but honestly, I don't think she's the assailant." She glanced over at him. "It may not sound logical, but as I mentioned before, I have the impression the person who whispered and grabbed at my arm is a man."

"I trust your instincts," he agreed. They quickly returned to the high school parking lot. So far, the trip to Madison had been less than fruitful.

Yet he was hopeful that returning to the ridge where he'd found Jacy may bring back some memories.

Based on how different things had looked to Jacy over time, he couldn't help but wonder if they should hold off heading back until darkness had fallen. Would the same time frame help jog her memory?

Or was this entire plan nothing more than a useless endeavor?

Cash reminded himself they needed to try.

"The girls who went missing after me, they all went to this high school, too?" Jacy asked.

"Two of them did, yes, but one of them went to a different one not far from here, Drake High School." He glanced at her. "We could drive past that building, too, if you think it would help."

Her brow puckered. "I was at Drake once, to attend a football game in the fall before the attack."

He thought back to the files he'd reviewed on the three women who'd disappeared. "I think Beth went to Drake."

"I guess we can drive past, but I don't see how that will jog my memory." She abruptly stopped and turned to face him. "Wait a minute, what if the attacker was a teacher? A substitute teacher might spend time at different high schools."

His pulse spiked. "That's a good thought. Do you remember any teachers that made you nervous or uncomfortable?"

"I barely remember the teachers at all," she said candidly. "But it can't be that hard to get a list of teachers who were on the payroll from the schools."

"Harder than you'd imagine," he said on a sigh. "I doubt they'll give me any personnel records without a warrant. I'll review Detective Ash's notes. Maybe she was able to obtain teacher information."

"Someone must have considered a teacher being involved," Jacy said. She stood near the passenger door, waiting for him to unlock the SUV. "We need to tell

Detective Vargas to check the schools Claire and Suzanna attended. Maybe the substitute teacher is back."

"Well, if so, then he or she couldn't have a criminal record. The schools check the background of every teacher on staff, even those who are substitutes."

"I hadn't thought of that." She sounded disappointed. "The nine-year gap between crimes is difficult to comprehend."

"We've assumed the perp was locked up, but maybe he just moved away." He was about to get into the SUV, but then glanced at the school. "I'm sure they keep yearbooks, here."

She did not look thrilled at the thought of going inside. But she closed her car door anyway, and came around to join him. "Okay, let's go."

He could sense her trepidation as they walked into the high school. It seemed so much smaller and insignificant than it had back when he was a student. The office was in the same location, though.

Cash pulled out his badge and flashed it at the woman seated behind the desk. "Detective Rawson, I'd like to speak to the principal about accessing yearbooks going back ten years."

"Ah, sure. But I don't think Principal Jordan is going to be any help," the woman said, rising to her feet.

"Surely they're not considered confidential," he protested.

"No, it's not that. But we had a fire about nine years ago. Destroyed all the old records we had on file, including the yearbooks."

"A fire?" he echoed in surprise. "What happened?"

"I'm not sure, but the fire department deemed it to be arson." She shrugged. "They never figured out who was responsible. Even the backup file on the computer was lost."

Cash glanced at Jacy, seeing the same shock in her eyes. There was no way that fire was a coincidence. He firmly believed the records had been destroyed on purpose.

SIX

Jacy followed Cash back out to the SUV, troubled by the news they'd received. "I don't understand, Cash. The fire doesn't make sense. I'm sure there are hundreds of students who still have their high school yearbooks. A fire wouldn't destroy them all."

"No, but the fire makes it more difficult to find the information we need." He unlocked the SUV so they could get inside. "We'll find a yearbook, but it's the personnel files themselves I'm wondering about. If your theory about the assailant being a substitute teacher is correct, we won't be able to prove he was here during the time frame of your attack."

She shivered, not because of the cold but the diabolical plan of the assailant. Nine years ago, he'd covered his tracks.

Now he was back.

"I really need to review Jane Ash's notes on the case," Cash muttered as he pulled out of the parking lot. "I can't believe she wouldn't have considered the fire at the school to be related to the missing girls."

She sighed and rubbed her temple. Fatigue and muscle soreness were dragging her down. Getting bad news didn't help. It wasn't easy to push away the discouragement. "Maybe we could grab something to eat and rest for a while."

"Sure." He shot her a concerned glance. "Are you feeling worse? Should I take you back to the ER?"

"No need." She waved her hand. "This is all taking more of an emotional toll than I anticipated."

Cash nodded. "I understand. Let's grab the phones, first. I want to touch base with Vargas about the fire."

"Sounds good. We may need more over-the-counter meds, too." She wasn't about to complain about getting a phone. Granted, this wouldn't be the same number, but it provided a way for her to make calls if needed.

A basic privilege she'd taken for granted until it was gone.

After they'd stopped at a discount store to get the phones and the ibuprofen, Cash drove to a family restaurant. The hostess seated them in a booth and a server came to take their order.

Jacy wasn't that hungry, but knew she had to eat something to give her strength. As she toyed with her water glass, she eyed Cash. "I think we should go to the ravine tonight, so that we are there at the exact same time you found me."

His brow creased. "Are you sure? It will be dark outside."

No, she wasn't sure of anything, but forced herself to nod. "I think it's best to recreate the actual scene, don't you? As I mentioned, the environment looks different by daylight."

"Okay, if you're up to it." He reached across the table to take her hand. "I'll be with you the entire time."

"I know." Being stuck with Cash like this hadn't

been something she'd planned, but there was no doubt that he'd do whatever was necessary to protect her. His warm fingers encircled hers, giving her wordless support and strength. Making her feel as if she could do anything with Cash at her side.

It was difficult to believe his former fiancée had let him go. He was handsome, sweet and protective.

Dedicated to his job, sure, but that was an admirable trait. Not something to get upset over.

When their server returned with their meals, she tugged her hand free, but Cash didn't let go. He waited for their server to leave before bowing his head. "Dear Lord, we thank You for keeping us safe in Your care. Please continue to guide us to the truth, and keep those missing women safe in Your care, too. Amen."

"Amen," she whispered, touched by his prayer.

Their fingers clung for a moment before he released her. "I feel certain we're on the right path, Jacy."

"I hope so." She didn't feel nearly as confident, especially in her ability to remember anything useful for the investigation, but she was willing to do her part. Even if it wasn't much. "It's nice to feel safe for a few hours."

"I can agree with that," he murmured. "I still don't like the fact that we were found in the Jeep loaned to us by Vargas."

"I think the assailant was staked out at the police station. Either way, it's done now. No sense in dwelling on it." In truth, she didn't want to think about how close she'd come to being dragged off by the assailant.

Twice.

She took a bite of her grilled chicken sandwich. The scent of french fries brought her appetite back.

"I think it's better if we find a motel outside the

city," Cash said, breaking into her thoughts. "I'd rather stay away from downtown Madison."

"Whatever you think is best." She frowned, thinking about how he'd purchased the phones and the over-the-counter pain meds. "I can pay for my motel room, too. No need for you to foot the bill for everything."

"I'll gladly take care of it," he quickly assured her. "You're doing me a favor by being here."

"Not just for you, Cash. For the missing girls." She munched a fry. "It bothers me to think that if I could have remembered who attacked me, the other women would still be alive and well."

"You are not to blame," Cash said firmly. "The assailant is the person responsible here. Not you, or the missing girls."

Easy to say, but virtually impossible to believe. Responsibility for their lives weighed heavily on her shoulders.

"God will guide us, Jacy." Cash searched her face. "You'll see."

"I hope so." She ate another french fry, trying to push the depressing thoughts of the victims aside. Cash was right about one thing. She needed to do everything possible to find the person responsible for these heinous crimes.

Less than an hour later, they were back in the SUV. Cash pulled up a listing of local hotels in the area, scrolling until he found one that he liked.

"How about this one?" He tapped the screen. "The Red Circle Inn."

"Fine with me." She glanced at the dashboard clock. "I can't believe it's almost three o'clock in the afternoon."

"You can rest while I follow up with the detectives." He smiled. "I remember I saw you running across the road at seven thirty in the evening."

She nodded. "Choir practice finished at seven o'clock. It was a five-minute walk to the Colgate house. That leaves almost twenty-five minutes before you caught a glimpse of me running across the road. I guess that means I managed to escape shortly after he grabbed me. I just wish I could remember how."

"All in good time, Jacy." He reached over to take her hand. "Tonight, we'll see if retracing those steps doesn't help break through the barrier around your memory."

She forced a smile, wishing she felt nearly as confident. "Let's hope so."

The motel was small and, based on the single car parked in front of one room, not very busy. Cash had her wait in the SUV while he secured two connecting rooms.

It was probably a good thing the place was so quiet. When Cash returned, he parked at the end of the row of rooms, then handed her a key.

He hauled their bags inside, including the recent phone purchases. Once they were settled, he went about activating and powering up the new phones.

While waiting, she pulled out her portfolio. Sitting on the bed, with the pillows propped behind her back, she went through the second half of her sketches, trying to imagine one of these perps coming back to seek revenge on her.

To her dismay, she only remembered about half of their names. Good thing she hadn't tried to become a cop or detective, she'd have failed miserably in those roles.

She put the drawings in two piles, the ones with names and those without. Seeing Felicia's sketch made her wonder if the Appleton PD had found her yet.

Cash rapped lightly on the door frame between their rooms before coming inside. "Hey, your phone is ready to go."

"Thanks." She took the device, feeling a measure of relief to have a connection with the outside world. "You mentioned I could check my email and let the precincts know I'm temporarily out of touch?"

"Yes, I have my computer set up on the table in my room." He gestured toward the drawings. "Looks like you've been busy."

"I don't remember them all," she admitted, scooting off the bed to join him. Yet another way her memory failed her.

It only took a moment for her to log into her email account. Thankfully, she didn't have any urgent messages waiting for a response. She quickly drafted an email to the contacts within each of the precincts she did work for, letting them know she was out of town, but could be reached via a new and hopefully temporary number if needed.

"I'm not sure we'll be able to leave Madison at the drop of a hat," Cash said from behind her, obviously reading her message.

"I can't just leave them high and dry. Besides, I'm sure they'll only reach out for urgent needs."

"Finding criminals is always urgent," he said dryly.

She turned on the chair to face him. "This is my career, Cash. I worked hard to establish myself as a credible and competent forensic artist. I can't just turn my back on the various police departments who depend on my skills."

"Okay, I hear you." He raised his hands in surrender. "But don't forget, we're roughly two hours away."

"I know." She stared down at the new phone in her lap. "I'm not sure who I am without my career."

"Hey, you're more than just a job," he protested. He moved the phone and drew her upright. "You're a beautiful, talented woman, Jacy."

She flushed at his words. "I wasn't fishing for a compliment. It's just that being out of touch made me realize how much of my sense of self is wrapped up in my career." She shook her head. "You pointed out earlier that I don't even bother to take vacations."

He gently tugged her close. "Maybe once we get to the bottom of these attacks, you'll find there is more to life than your job. Which is very important, don't get me wrong. I've been focused on my career, too." He pressed a kiss to the top of her head. "Once the danger is over, you should consider attending church with me. Or even better, consider joining a church choir."

She pulled back to look up at him. Maybe he was right that she needed to broaden her horizons a bit. She'd been so focused on helping to bring criminals to justice and building her career that she hadn't made time for other things.

Like having a personal life.

Granted, Greg's cheating had soured her on dating. After that debacle, she hadn't thought much about finding a guy.

Until now.

"I'll think about that, thanks." It wasn't as if she

didn't have friends among the cops she worked with, because she did. None, however, who were really close.

None she could turn to in a time like this.

Cash's gaze clung to hers for a long moment. Then his eyes lowered to her mouth. She went still, anticipating his kiss. But his phone rang, the jarring sound pulling them apart.

"Sorry about that." He looked disappointed as he reached for his phone. "Vargas? Thanks for calling me back."

She took a shaky step back, wondering what in the world she was thinking. Kissing Cash was not smart. For one thing, they lived in different cities. And he saw her as a way to close a case, nothing more. She knew full well that once this was over, they'd go their separate ways.

She turned away, knowing she'd miss him when their time together ended.

"I'm sorry, could you repeat that?" Cash felt like an idiot for being so focused on his plan to kiss Jacy that he'd completely missed what the older detective had said.

"Do we have a bad connection?" Vargas asked a bit impatiently. "We have Felicia Gephardt in custody. She took off to stay with a friend in Milwaukee, so she's in violation of her parole, which is good news for us. The bad news is that she has been in Milwaukee for over forty-eight hours, so there's no way she's Jacy's assailant."

"Oh, ah, that's good." He really needed to pull himself together. "I mean, I wish it was that easy, but at least we can cross her off the suspect list."

"Are you okay?" Vargas asked. "You sound distracted."

Yeah, that was one way to put it. Jacy was a big-time distraction. "I'm fine. There's been no sign of a tail. I think we're safe here."

"I won't ask where, because I know you want to stay off-grid," Vargas said wryly. "Thanks for calling to give me your new number, though. And what's this about a fire at Jacy's former high school?"

Cash quickly filled Vargas in on the information they'd gleaned. The detective was interested in the substitute teacher angle, admitting it would not be unusual for a temp to fill in at multiple schools.

"I'll create a list of substitute teachers for the high school here in Appleton," Vargas said. "It can't hurt."

"I agree, it's something." He didn't want to tell Vargas their plan to head to the ravine. "If we learn anything else, I'll let you know."

"Same goes." Vargas paused then added, "Keep an eye on Jacy. I don't like the way she's become a target."

"I will," he promised. "Later."

After he'd finished his call, Jacy glanced at him. "I knew it wasn't Felicia."

"Yeah, one down and far too many suspects to go," he said with a sigh.

"I'll let you get back to work." Jacy moved through the connecting doors. "Let me know when you're ready to head out to the crime scene."

Letting her go wasn't easy, but he had work to do. He took the chair she'd vacated and began searching online for yearbooks. It didn't take long to find one from the year Jacy was attacked being offered for sale at a reasonable price.

He made a note of the address, deciding to stop there on the way over to the ravine. If Jacy was right about the perp being a substitute teacher, it wasn't likely the yearbook would be much help. But he couldn't afford to ignore any leads, no matter how small.

Next, he went through Detective Ash's entire report, disappointed to note she hadn't considered the teacher angle. Or, if she had, she hadn't made any notes about it.

He worked until six o'clock, then forced himself to shut down the computer. It was easy to get lost in the details of the investigation, especially since the few tidbits Jacy had remembered hadn't been included in Ash's notes.

Jane Ash was a good detective, but he found himself wishing she'd documented her findings better. Not that he was perfect, by any means. But looking back, it was difficult to know if Jacy remembered new things or if Ash just hadn't made note of them. No doubt she'd been reassigned to other cases once this one had gone cold.

It wasn't cold now, he thought grimly. Just the opposite. It was molten hot. If the assailant coming for Jacy was the same one who'd taken her ten years ago.

If not, then he was certain the assailant targeting Jacy had also been involved in Claire's and Suzanna's disappearances. A copycat? Maybe.

"What time do you want to leave?"

He glanced over to see Jacy hovering in the connecting doorway of their rooms. "Now is good. I'm sure we'll hit traffic along the way."

"What if the ridge isn't there anymore?" She ventured farther into the room. "Seeing all the new developments makes me think that the wooded field with a steep ravine could be a subdivision by now."

"It's not a subdivision. I checked the area out not long ago." Specifically, the day before he'd decided to drive up to Appleton to meet Jacy. "There are some developments going up nearby, though, so it's only a matter of time until the area is built over."

"Well, then, I guess it's a good thing we're heading there now." Her smile didn't quite reach her eyes.

Jacy was brave, and as bad as he felt about putting her through this, it absolutely needed to be done. He pushed away from the small table and reached for his coat. "Ready?"

"Yes." This time she sounded more positive.

He led the way outside. The car that had been there before was gone now, making the motel look completely empty. Except, of course, for their two rooms.

"Did you find anything interesting?" Jacy asked as he left the parking lot.

"I found someone selling a copy of your yearbook, and we might want to swing by there on our way back." He'd spent too much time on the computer to go there now. "And I found George Voight."

"Who?" She stared at him blankly.

"He and his wife lived in the Colgate house. His wife passed away, but he's in an assisted-living apartment in Madison." He shrugged. "I think we should pay him a visit tomorrow."

"Yeah, okay. Although, like I said, I doubt his memory has improved over time."

He decided not to mention the missing details in the case file. Thankfully, Jane Ash had noted the names of the neighbors who'd been interviewed, but he'd noticed that only Martha, George's wife, had issued a statement.

No one had gone back to follow up with George, to see if he'd seen or heard anything. Or if they had, no notes had been made about that conversation.

They were roughly five minutes early when he pulled off at the side of a rural highway. He threw the SUV in gear then turned toward Jacy. "I was on my way home from work when I saw you running. I slowed down, fearing you were going to race right across the road without stopping. And you did. I pulled over right here to follow you."

She glanced around the area, her brow furrowed in a grimace. "I don't see any houses or anything nearby."

"I know. Detective Ash searched the area for a place where you may have been held against your will, but didn't find anything." He watched her for a moment. "Do you remember being in a car or at a house?"

"No. I don't remember running this way at all." She pushed open her door. "Let's see if walking this way brings back any memories."

He didn't hesitate to join her in the blustery air. The darkness brought a damp chill, especially as the wind kicked up. He moved forward to show Jacy the way.

The landscape was dotted with snow, much like it had been that night. It wasn't as cold tonight, though. After about fifty yards, they climbed a slight incline and then stopped at the top of the hill.

"I must not have noticed the ravine," Jacy said in a low voice. "This hill has a very steep decline here."

"I yelled a warning, but you were already rolling down the slope." He remembered fearing she was dead.

Jacy began making her way down the steep slope.

He followed behind, just as he heard what sounded like a muffled gunshot. A silencer? He felt something strike his upper arm.

"Down! Get down!" he cried hoarsely, throwing himself on top of her.

The assailant had found them!

SEVEN

Cash's heavy weight pushed her to the ground, but then he rolled off her as they both tumbled down the incline. She scrabbled for a handhold, but found nothing to break her fall.

Was this how she'd ended up at the bottom of the ravine ten years ago? The jarring movement felt worse on her already sore and battered muscles.

When she finally stopped moving, she was on her back, staring up at the starry sky. Had there been stars out that night, too? Why couldn't she remember?

"Jacy?" Cash's voice was hoarse. He crawled toward her, his expression panicked. "Are you okay? You weren't hit by the dart?"

In the darkness, she could just make out the dart that was imbedded at an angle in the sleeve of his coat. Pushing herself upright, she reached for it. "Do you feel funny? Did the dart inject anything into your bloodstream?"

"I don't think so." He stared at the dart in her fingers then reached inside his jacket to feel his arm. There didn't seem to be any injection sight. "The tip of the dart must not have penetrated my leather coat. The angle is such that it went sideways through the leather rather than into me."

"I'm so glad," she whispered. What if Cash had been drugged? She wouldn't have been strong enough to get him out of harm's way.

"We need to find cover." He took the dart and carefully put it in his pocket. They were both lying flat on the ground, but she knew they were still vulnerable if the shooter came to find them. "You first, Jacy. I'll cover you from behind. Crawl on your belly toward those trees, okay?"

She nodded, her heart lodged in her throat. They were both wearing dark clothing, but that wasn't enough to prevent the assailant from finding them. Crawling on her belly meant dragging herself over the rocky damp ground, but she ignored the mud. Keeping her eyes on the trees that were roughly twenty yards away from their current location, she moved as quickly as possible, praying the assailant wouldn't shoot another dart at Cash.

After an incredibly long ten minutes, she reached the trees. She pushed herself up, but Cash put a restraining hand on her shoulder. "No, I need you to stay down."

She fell back onto her stomach, turning so she could view the ridge. Scanning the area along the top, she didn't see anyone lurking there with a gun.

Had the assailant run off? Or was he biding his time, waiting to shoot again?

There was the barest hint of movement along the top of the ridge. A head poked up and then she saw the tip of a rifle.

"Gun!" she croaked.

Cash had pulled his own weapon, too. He fired off

a round just as another feathered dart landed in a tree, mere inches from him.

In that instant it was clear the assailant wanted to neutralize Cash to get to her!

The gun at the top of the ridge disappeared. Maybe Cash had hit him?

"Call 9-1-1," Cash said, staring toward the top of the ridge. "I want backup, ASAP!"

Fumbling for her new phone, she made the call. The emergency operator asked for her location, and all she could provide was an approximation, adding that their SUV was along the side of the road. She mentally kicked herself for not paying attention to any highway markers along the way.

"There's no sign of him," Cash muttered. "I wish I could take off after him. I don't want this guy to escape justice!"

She reached out to grab the edge of his jacket. "Don't leave me here."

"I won't." He gave her a quick, reassuring smile, before turning back to peer at the ridge. "But it's beyond frustrating to know he'll get away with this."

Frustration was putting it mildly. This guy had tried to neutralize Cash with a tranquilizer gun, twice. It was difficult to comprehend how they'd managed to get away.

Unless Cash was right about God watching over them. Humbling to realize it was the only explanation she could come up with for how the dart had gotten stuck within his leather jacket rather than going into his shoulder.

"I don't see any movement along the ridge, do you?" Cash asked.

"No." She swallowed hard. "I'm sure he's long gone."

"Yeah." Cash's tone rang with disgust. He turned to look at her. "This is my fault, Jacy. I should have anticipated the assailant would stake out the ravine."

"It's not your fault, Cash. There's no way we could have known this would happen."

"Yeah, but the fact that you escaped the assailant ten years ago, ending up right here, is key." He turned to stare at the ridge again then reached up and took the dart out of the tree, putting it in his pocket with the other one. "I'm more convinced than ever that the assailant who took you ten years ago is the same one coming after you now."

The same assailant. She didn't want to believe it, but the way this guy had showed up here, where it all started, was impossible to ignore.

The sound of police sirens filled the night air. The hour wasn't late, but the darkness made it feel as if it was after midnight.

When they could see the red and blue lights flashing over the top of the ridge, Cash rose to his feet. He gave her a hand up and then surprised her by pulling her tightly against him.

"I'm so glad you're safe," he whispered against her hair.

"Ditto," she managed to sigh, burying her face against his neck.

They clung to each other for a long moment. She didn't want to let him go, but knew the cops were there, searching for them.

She lifted her head to look up at him. They stared at each other for a long moment, but while she anticipated his kiss, he turned away. She swallowed the stab of disappointment.

"Here," Cash shouted, turning to walk toward the hill. He kept his arm around her waist. "We're here!"

Two officers appeared up top, the beams from their flashlights raking over them. "Detective Rawson?"

"Yeah. And this is Jacy Urban." He turned to her. "Do you think you can get back up to the top?"

"Yes." She hugged him then stepped away to begin the climb.

Going up wasn't nearly as easy as falling down. The damp earth from areas of melted snow made her slip several times.

When she finally got near the top, the police officer closest to her helped pull her the rest of the way. The other cop did the same with Cash.

"What happened?" The officer raked his scrutiny over their muddy clothes. "Did you fall down the hill?"

"We were shot at twice by a perp with a tranquilizer gun." Cash pulled the two darts from his coat pocket. "Thankfully, neither of us was drugged by whatever is inside these darts."

The two officers looked at each other in surprise. "I never heard of anyone being shot with a tranq gun," one said.

"Here, let's take those as evidence." The other officer tucked the flashlight under his arm to pull out an evidence bag. Cash dropped the darts inside. "Sorry, I had to handle them."

"It's fine, we'll get them tested at the lab." The cop tucked the evidence bag away. "I don't suppose either of you got a good look at the perp?"

"No. I took a shot at him, though." Cash held out

his hand for the flashlight. The officer handed it over and he aimed the light along the top of the ridge. He walked the entire area then heaved a sigh. "There's no blood trail. I must have missed."

"Hey, we'll get something off the darts," the officer assured him.

"Yeah, maybe." Cash didn't look convinced. She understood his concern. So far, the assailant had been wearing gloves during every attack. No reason to think tonight's attempt was any different.

"We'd like you to come down to the station to give a statement." The officers stood side by side. "We can give you a lift if you'd like."

Cash glanced at her and gestured toward the SUV. "If you don't mind, we'll use our own vehicle."

"Okay." The officers turned away.

Cash took her hand as they made their way to the SUV. When they reached it, he abruptly stopped and frowned.

"What's wrong?" The SUV looked fine to her.

He dragged his hand through his hair. "We'll need to swap rides again. I can't risk this guy having our license plate number."

"Maybe we should ride with the cops."

He shook his head. "I doubt the assailant is anywhere nearby. He's long gone by now. But once we're finished giving our statements, we'll need a different set of wheels."

"Okay." She pulled open the passenger's-side door, feeling exhausted. The aches and pains from tumbling down the hill were minor compared to the feeling of despair that threatened to overwhelm her.

No matter how hard she tried, her memory remained

stubbornly blocked. Jacy had very little hope of re-membering anything that would help put this guy be-hind bars.

And save the lives of the missing teenagers.

Guilt rode his back like an angry gorilla. Cash knew he shouldn't have underestimated the assailant, but he had mistakenly believed the assailant was still back in Appleton.

Not waiting for them here in Madison, at the scene of the original crime.

Giving their statements to one of his colleagues, Detective Hank Singleton, didn't take long. When they finished, Cash was able to convince an officer to give them a ride to their motel, using the back door of the precinct to avoid being followed. It was too late to get another rental vehicle. And from the way Jacy was shivering in her damp clothes, a hot shower was more important.

"I'm going to order a pizza," he said when they were back at the motel. "Anything in particular you don't like?"

"I'm fine with everything except anchovies." She looked pale and fragile in the dim light.

"I can work with that," he assured her. He watched as she disappeared into her room then turned to put in the order. When that was finished, he took a quick shower, too. Changing into clean and dry clothes felt wonderful.

While he waited for Jacy and their pizza, he opened the laptop. He'd found George Voight's address and his location using a map app. Tonight had been a colossal failure, but he was determined to keep pushing forward.

Giving up wasn't an option.

The pizza arrived fifteen minutes later. Cash paid the kid, adding a nice tip, and set the pizza on the table. There was no sound from Jacy's room, so he tentatively approached the connecting door.

"Jacy?" He rapped on the frame.

No answer.

"Are you okay?" He took a quick peek inside, but the room was empty. A flash of panic hit hard, until he noticed the bathroom door was closed.

Her sketch pad was on the bed, but her overnight bag was missing. She'd probably taken it into the bathroom with her.

He'd turned to head back to his room when the partially finished sketch caught his eye. He stepped closer, his eyes widening in surprise when he realized Jacy had sketched him.

She'd made him look more handsome than he was; he knew his nose was too prominent and his hair a little too long and scruffy. But he was impressed by her skill just the same.

The bathroom door opened, startling him. He hastened toward the connecting door. "Sorry," he called. "Didn't mean to invade your privacy."

"No worries, I'm decent."

He glanced over his shoulder in time to see her drop her bag on the bed. She flushed when she realized he'd seen her drawing.

"You do amazing work, Jacy."

"I was just practicing." She brushed off his compliment, even though clearly her job of sketching bad guys had resulted in several arrests. "Is the pizza here?"

"Yep, please come join me." He gestured for her to follow him into the room.

"Oh, I'm glad you got some bottled water, too." She reached for one, twisted off the cap and took a long drink. "Thank you."

She shouldn't be thanking him for almost getting her killed. Once they were seated, he reached for her hand. "We need to thank God for keeping us safe, tonight."

"Yes, we do," she agreed.

"Dear Lord, we thank You for providing us safety tonight against those who seek to do us harm. We also ask that You continue to watch over the missing girls, Claire and Suzanna. Please provide us the strength and wisdom we need to find them, in Jesus's name, Amen."

"Amen," she whispered. "Oh, Cash, I really wish we could find those poor girls."

"Me, too." Thinking of the two teenage girls put a damper on his appetite, but he did his best to dig into the pizza, knowing he needed the sustenance to keep Jacy safe.

A task he'd nearly failed at. If that dart had impaled his skin, he'd probably have fallen unconscious, leaving Jacy alone and vulnerable.

Exactly as the assailant had intended.

The pizza tasted like sawdust, but he chewed and swallowed, anyway. He was relieved to see Jacy was eating, too. This had been an incredibly long day, filled with danger from early this morning until tonight.

Despite his failures, they were safe now.

They ate in silence for a few minutes before Jacy sighed.

"I'm sorry my memory hasn't returned." She frowned, adding, "I think it's time to try hypnosis again."

He eyed her thoughtfully. "That might help. Especially if you're determined to break through your buried memories."

"I have always wanted that," she snapped. But her anger quickly faded. "You're probably right about me subconsciously resisting the hypnosis. At the time, I was young and scared. I'd like to believe I'm older and wiser, now."

"Hey, I don't blame you, Jacy." He patted her hand. "I can only imagine how difficult this has been for you."

"But those other women…" Her voice trailed off. "I'm afraid they're dead, Cash. And that hurts more than anything."

He'd always suspected they were dead, but hadn't wanted to put additional pressure on her by mentioning it. To his mind, the fact that Jacy had managed to get away had caused this guy to make sure the others he grabbed never did.

He was no psychologist, but the way the teenage girls all looked the same was definitely a big part of this perp's MO. Cash didn't doubt that this assailant was looking for a Jacy replacement.

And wouldn't be satisfied until he had Jacy in his clutches again.

He cleared his throat, tearing himself from those grim thoughts. "We need to think positive, Jacy. To have hope that we'll find them alive and unharmed."

"I pray you're right." She stared down at her pizza for a long moment then lifted her green eyes to his. "We need to find someone to hypnotize me first thing in the morning. The more I think about it, I wish we had done that already."

That might not be as easy as it sounded, but he nodded. "We'll get a replacement vehicle then stop by to visit George Voight. Once those two things are done, we'll find someone to do the hypnosis."

"Good." She gave a tiny nod. "I know you thought going over the scene would help, but it hasn't. I think it's time we take more drastic measures."

He arched a brow. "We're doing our best here. Let's stay the course, okay?"

"That's not good enough." She jerked away from the table and turned to pace the room. "There has to be more we can do, Cash." She shoved her hands through her hair.

"We're going to find him."

She whirled to face him. "I know that's what you believe, but it's not happening fast enough. Not when two young girls are missing. If we don't stop him, he'll keep coming after me, or worse, he'll grab another girl!"

"Hey, don't torture yourself over this." He stood and crossed to her. "Please, Jacy, I know this has been a difficult day, but none of this is your fault."

"Really? Then why does it feel like it's my fault?" Her tormented gaze clung to his. "Why do I get the impression that if this guy had killed me ten years ago, these other women would be alive and living with their families, rather than missing with their whereabouts unknown?"

He pulled her into his arms. "You're taking on way too much responsibility. None of this is your fault. You didn't cause this guy's obsession. You should know that most serial killers aren't satisfied with only one victim. Even if you had died that night ten years ago, I highly doubt he'd have stopped."

"I hate thinking I may have contributed to his obsession," she whispered.

"You didn't cause this," he repeated, aching for her. "I know it's hard not to take this situation personally, but his twisted mind is not your fault."

She rested against him for a long moment. When she lifted her head, their eyes clung, the same way they had when they were out on the ridge.

He'd wanted so badly to kiss her, but hearing the cops coming toward them had been a distraction.

There was no such distraction now.

"Cash?" Jacy's voice was low and husky. Then she reached up on her tippy toes and kissed him.

He instinctively pulled her closer, kissing her back, the way he'd longed to do since reconnecting with her. For a long moment, there was nothing but Jacy, but then she pulled away and stepped back.

"I—uh, sorry. I don't know what I was thinking." She avoided his eyes. "I'm not hungry anymore. I should get some rest. Good night, Cash."

"Jacy, wait…" But she was already across the room and through the connecting door.

He jammed his fingers through his hair, wondering if he'd come on too strong.

Or if she'd only kissed him out of gratitude, while he'd secretly longed for something more.

EIGHT

Kissing Cash was a big mistake. Jacy covered her heated cheeks with her hands, her gaze landing on the sketch she'd done of him. With an inward groan, she picked up the pad and flipped the pages to hide the image from view.

There was no point in thinking about Cash Rawson on a personal level. This weird closeness wasn't normal. They had come to Madison to find the assailant who'd taken several teenage girls from their homes.

Falling for a handsome detective was out of the question. They had different lives, in different cities.

Once this guy was caught and arrested, their paths wouldn't cross again.

Besides, Jacy was leery of dating another cop. True, Greg's cheating didn't mean other officers would, but after they'd broken up, she'd decided it would be better to find someone outside law enforcement to spend time with.

That, however, was a project for another day. Impossible to think of having a personal relationship when running from an assailant.

Jacy washed up then crawled into bed. But sleep

didn't come easily. The events of the day, the early morning smoke bomb and the near miss on the ridge replayed in her mind.

And now they needed to rent a different car. She stared up at the ceiling, wondering if she shouldn't just use herself as bait to catch this guy.

After all, she was the one he wanted. Horrifying to see firsthand how this fiend would have hurt or killed Cash in his quest to get to her.

Her thoughts refused to settle, so she prayed for peace and rest. The next thing she knew, light filtered through the opening between the curtains.

The hours of sleep helped her to feel refreshed, although her muscles were still stiff and sore when she rolled out of the bed. Apparently tumbling down the hill to the bottom of the ravine had only added to her previous aches and pains.

A hot shower helped, as did a couple of ibuprofens. When she crossed over to the connecting door, she heard Cash speaking to someone. Curious, she pushed the door open to step inside.

His glance caught hers and his warm smile knocked her off balance.

Not that she'd ever been on balance around Cash.

"Thanks, Vargas. Keep us posted." He lowered the phone and stood. "You look great."

The compliment warmed her cheeks. "I—uh, it's amazing what getting a few hours of sleep can do. What did Vargas want?"

"I called to fill him in on the incident last night at the ravine." Cash grimaced. "I wanted to make sure he was in the loop on everything that's been happening, since the attacks started in his jurisdiction. He was going to talk to Detective Hank Singleton, so they can compare notes on this guy. Maybe between the two of them, we'll learn something new."

"That would be good." She eyed the leftover cold pizza. "Is that breakfast?"

He looked chagrined. "It works for me, and I still have chips, too, if you're interested. But if you'd like real breakfast food, we can stop somewhere after we rent a replacement vehicle."

She managed a wan smile as she sat beside him. "No need, cold pizza is fine. We shouldn't waste food, anyway."

"A woman after my own heart," he teased. Then he took her hand in his. "Dear Lord, we thank You for keeping us safe in Your care. We ask that You bless this food we are about to eat and to continue guiding us on Your chosen path to the truth. Amen."

"Amen," she echoed. She picked up a slice of pizza and took a bite. "Not bad."

"What? The prayer or the pizza?" He seemed to be in a lighthearted mood. Maybe getting a few hours' sleep had been healing for him, too.

"Both. All I need is some coffee."

"Coming right up." He jumped to his feet and made a fresh cup for her. When he returned, she gratefully accepted it.

"Thanks." When he sat beside her again, she said, "I think we need to set me up in a place where the assailant can find me."

Cash choked as his coffee went down the wrong pipe. "What?" he said between hacking coughs. "No way!"

"Do you need the Heimlich?" she asked with an arched brow.

"No!" He coughed again. "But we're not setting you up as bait, Jacy. No way, no how."

She'd had a feeling he wouldn't like her idea. "Just hear me out, Cash."

"No. Not happening." He shook his head and drank from his water bottle to soothe his throat. "We'll find this guy using old-fashioned detective work. Too many things could go wrong with trying to set a trap for him."

She groaned and ate another bite of cold pizza. "It's not as if things haven't already gone wrong, Cash. He seems to know our every move."

"Look, Jacy, I understand your frustration. I really do." He turned in his seat and took both of her hands in his, giving her an imploring stare. "But I need you to work with me here. If we can find a way to unlock your memories, we'll be able to mobilize every police force from Madison all the way to Appleton to find him."

"I've tried that," she protested. "It's time to take more drastic action."

"Not setting you up as bait," he said firmly. "Let's finish up here, and see if we can't get the desk clerk to call a taxi. We'll rent a different car then head over to speak with George Voight."

She did not have one iota of hope that George would remember anything significant from ten years ago, but they did need a vehicle to get around. She decided to drop the subject of setting herself up to draw out the assailant.

For now.

When they'd finished polishing off the remains of their pizza, she headed over to her room to gather her things. After tucking her portfolio and her sketch pad into her bag, she returned to Cash's room.

"I'll take that for you." He reached for her bag. "Let's walk over to chat with the lobby clerk."

She stayed back as Cash checked out of their rooms and requested a taxi. Within ten minutes, they were back on the road, heading to the closest rental car agency.

"What about the other SUV?" she asked in a hushed tone.

"I'll pay to have it towed back to Appleton." She winced, anticipating the cost, but he simply shrugged. "Better that, than to be caught by the assailant again."

By the time they navigated the morning traffic and secured a replacement vehicle, it was nine thirty. When Cash entered the address for George Voight's assisted-living complex, she wanted to groan when she noticed it was located on the other side of the city.

"I don't know how you stand this traffic," she muttered. "I'll take Appleton over this mess any day."

"I'm used to it." He wedged his way between two cars, earning a honk from an irritated driver. "It's not as bad as Chicago."

"That's true. I was only there for the six-month forensic artist training course and remember being glad I didn't have a car at the time. It was a fun place to visit, but I had no desire to live there."

Thirty minutes later, Cash finally pulled into the parking lot of George's building. She and Cash walked inside and found his apartment number. When Cash leaned on the buzzer, there was no response for a long moment.

"Who is this?" a cranky voice finally answered.

"Detective Rawson with the Madison PD," Cash answered. "I'm sorry to bother you, Mr. Voight, but I'd like to ask you a few questions."

"Harrumph." For a moment, Jacy thought he would tell them to get lost, but the elderly man unlocked the door so they could head upstairs.

They took the elevator since the Voight apartment was on the eighth floor. Cash strode down the hall and lightly knocked on the man's door.

"It's Detective Rawson," Cash repeated. "I'm here with Jacy Urban."

The door opened, revealing a tall, thin man with stooped shoulders and tuffs of gray hair around his ears. "Who?" he demanded, eyeing her with suspicion.

"This is Jacy Urban. She was abducted ten years ago, but managed to escape."

George glowered but stepped back. "Come in, then," he said grudgingly.

"Thank you." Cash took her arm, drawing her forward. The apartment was about the same size as hers, although the kitchen seemed smaller.

"What's this about?" George demanded once they were all seated in the living room.

"Ten years ago, you lived with your wife in a house on Corbin Lane," Cash said. "Located a few blocks from the high school."

"Yeah." George nodded. "I remember. That was before Martha passed away." He glanced around the room. "My kids thought I would be better off here."

"It's a very nice apartment," Jacy said quickly.

"They offer three meals a day, so that's nice." George shrugged. "I was never much of a cook."

"Did you ever speak to Detective Jane Ash about a

missing girl?" Cash asked. "I believe your wife may have spoken to her."

George looked thoughtful for a moment then nodded. "Yes, I remember now. A girl went missing, but was found. The police came to ask about what we saw."

Cash darted a quick look at Jacy. "But you didn't speak directly with Detective Ash, did you?"

"No, but I didn't see anyone getting kidnapped." George's eyes came to rest on her. "You were the girl that night?"

"Yes, I was," Jacy said. "And we have reason to believe other girls went missing over the next few months, and more recently, too, because of the same guy."

"That's not right. What is this world coming to?" George shook his head. "I wish I could help you, but I didn't see anyone. Although I remember seeing you, young lady. You stopped right in front of the house then turned back to talk to someone behind you."

A chill snaked down Jacy's spine. "I did?"

"Yep." George gave a firm nod. "You turned and headed back that way. I didn't see who you were talking to, though."

Jacy stared at him in shocked surprise. She didn't remember stopping in front of his house and turning to talk to someone behind her.

Did this mean she'd known the person who'd abducted her? Why couldn't she remember?

A surge of anticipation hit hard. Cash could barely keep himself from jumping up with excitement. George Voight had provided good information. Yeah, sure, he'd rather have a description that Jacy could work with, but he would take what he could get.

Especially since he could tell by Jacy's expression that she didn't remember anything about talking to someone on the sidewalk behind her that fateful night.

"Do you remember anything else?" Cash asked.

"Nah." George waved a hand. "I'm not even sure why I happened to look out the window that night. I didn't pay attention to the kids walking by, unless they were making a bunch of noise."

"So, after Jacy turned to walk back a few steps, you didn't hear anything? A scream? A cry for help?"

"Nothing," George grumbled. "I would have told someone if I'd heard a scream."

"I'm sure you would have," Jacy murmured, still looking shell-shocked. "Thanks for taking the time to talk to us."

"I wish I could be more help." George pushed himself to his feet. Cash and Jacy followed him to the door. "Sorry about what happened."

"I'm fine," Jacy assured him.

"Thanks again for your time," Cash added. He shook George's hand then left the apartment.

Jacy was silent as they rode the elevator down to the main level.

"I guess it's good we came," she finally said. "Apparently, I must have recognized the assailant."

"That's one theory, but it could also be that a stranger called out for help." He glanced at her. "You're the type of person who would not have hesitated to offer assistance."

"Maybe," she breathed. "We need to find someone to hypnotize me. Or we need to set a trap for this guy. I don't think I can take another day of driving around and waiting for him to make another attempt to hurt you and grab me."

"He doesn't know where we are." He was getting irritated with her determination to set herself up as bait. He struggled to keep his voice even. "I would ask that you trust me, Jacy. Please? I won't let this guy hurt you."

She whirled and stabbed him in the chest with her index finger. "I don't want him to hurt you, either, got it?"

His annoyance vanished and he fought a smile at her fierce tone. "Got it."

She threw up her hands. "Why does it feel like I'm talking to a rock?"

"I hear you, Jacy." He opened the passenger door for her. "We'll see if we can find a place for hypnosis, and maybe I will get my hands on your high school yearbook. Those are two good places to start."

She sighed and slid into the seat. "We need another place to stay, too."

"Yeah, I know." He was running low on finances, but didn't want to mention that to Jacy. This was his plan, not hers. He didn't expect her to fund it. His place wasn't too far, and he felt certain it was safe enough to stop by to replenish his resources.

Safe enough to spend the night? Maybe. This assailant had found them by going back to the original scene of the crime. Cash honestly didn't think the perp knew him by name.

Although the guy might assume he's a cop, based on the way he'd returned fire.

He pulled away from the assisted-living complex,

merging into traffic and then glancing at Jacy. "Would you be okay stopping at my place for a few things?"

She shrugged. "Sure. If you think it's safe, I'm all for it."

"Great." He gestured to the GPS in the dashboard. "See if you can find a place to do hypnosis."

She stared at it for a moment before reaching up to type with her index finger. "This seems odd, like we're going to end up with someone who does this out of their basement or garage."

"Okay, we can wait until we get to my place. I'll call the psychologist who works with the department. Maybe she'll have an idea."

Jacy groaned. "Pretty sure that same psychologist referred me to Melanie Bush ten years ago."

"You remember the name of the hypnotist?" He was surprised. "Why didn't you mention that? We can try her again."

"I think we should try someone else." Jacy spread her hands. "Nothing against Melanie, but it didn't work. My mind was too blocked. I never went under, despite how long she sat there talking, telling me to relax and take deep breaths."

"Okay, you're right. Starting over with someone new might be a good idea."

"I'll try my best to make it work," Jacy said in a low voice. "I really don't want to fail in this."

"No pressure, Jacy. Just do your best." He was concerned that the more emphasis she placed on this tactic and her ability, the more she'd subconsciously resist.

Not on purpose, of course. He was no expert, but the mind wasn't always logical.

He found it surprising that hypnosis hadn't worked,

though. He'd think a young girl would be more suscep-
tible to being hypnotized, but not in Jacy's case.

"Do you really think paging through my old yearbook will help?" Jacy's question brought him back to
the present. "I don't think substitute teachers are listed
there."

"I think we need to try. But I'm open to other ideas.
Except for the one where you try to lure the assailant
by yourself. That's not up for discussion."

"Like I want to put myself in harm's way?" Jacy
sounded exasperated. "It just seems like that's the
quickest way to find this guy. And I don't understand
why you won't even consider it as a possible plan."

He ground his teeth together but didn't answer. For
one thing, he cared about Jacy too much to use her like
that. Besides, the police didn't use civilians to draw
out bad guys.

But they did sometimes use other cops as decoys.

"I'll talk to my boss, see if we can't find a female
cop who fits the assailant's preferred target."

She sighed. "Okay, but that might take time. Easier
for me to take on the role."

Since that wasn't an option, he didn't bother to respond. They drove the rest of the way to his small house
in silence. Property was expensive in Madison, but he'd
found a fixer-upper four years ago and had been slowly
renovating the place.

There was still some work to do but, overall, it
looked much better than when he'd bought it. He pulled
into the driveway, sweeping his eyes around the area
to make sure there was nothing amiss.

The place looked exactly the way he'd left it forty-eight hours ago. He stepped from the driver's side and went around to unlock the front door.

Jacy was behind him when he pushed the door open and walked inside. He narrowed his eyes, abruptly stopped and pulled his weapon.

"Stay back!" He spoke in a hushed whisper, gripping his service weapon tightly.

"What's wrong?" Jacy gripped the back of his leather jacket.

The interior of his house looked fine, but he was keenly aware that his personal things had been moved around, slightly out of place. Someone had been there.

Cash hesitated, torn between keeping Jacy with him, and sending her back to the car. In the end, he whispered, "Stick close."

"Okay," she whispered.

He eased through the living area to the kitchen. After clearing that space, he turned to head down the hall to the bedrooms.

The hair on the back of his neck lifted in alarm when he saw the door to his room was closed. Normally, he left it open.

His gut jangled in warning. He quickly turned, pulling Jacy along with him to leave the house just as gunfire erupted from the bedroom.

Two bullets blasted through the door, whizzing past and missing them by inches!

NINE

The loud retort of gunfire reverberated through the house as Cash dragged her outside.

"Get in the car!"

She was already wrenching open the passenger's-side door. Cash didn't waste a second in sliding behind the wheel. He started the car, threw the gear in Reverse and shot out of the driveway into the street.

Jacy turned in her seat to check behind them. A tall figure wearing all black and a face mask ran out into the road, still holding a gun.

"He's going to shoot again!" The sound of two more rounds of gunfire punctuated her shout.

Amazingly, the bullets didn't hit their vehicle. Cash careened around a corner then punched the gas to shoot down the street.

Moments later, they were taking an on-ramp to the interstate. Jacy swallowed hard, her heart still hammering in her chest. "Where are we going?"

"I don't know." Cash's expression could have been carved in granite. "Another motel far from here, that's for sure. I never anticipated he'd be at my place, waiting for us."

"I don't blame you." She drew in a calming breath. "If not for your quick actions in getting us out of there, this would have ended much differently."

"We shouldn't have been there in the first place. It burns to know I underestimated this guy." Cash thumped his hand on the steering wheel. "I can't believe he was hiding in the bedroom. That he knows my name, found my house and knows that I'm protecting you."

The realization was sobering.

"I need to call this in," Cash said, speaking more to himself, she thought, than to her.

"I'll call." She pulled out her disposable phone and frowned. "Do I dial 9-1-1?"

"I'm sure my neighbors have already reported the gunfire," Cash said. "Call this number, then hand me your phone."

She did as he instructed, giving him the phone.

"Lieutenant Timmons? This is Rawson. An assailant was hiding in my house and began shooting at us. We managed to get away, but I want the place combed for evidence. I don't know how long he was hiding in my bedroom, but it's possible he left DNA behind, along with several shell casings."

Jacy couldn't hear the other side of the conversation. After a long moment, Cash continued, "Yes, Jacy Urban has been targeted by several attacks over the past two days. We have reason to believe this most recent gunfire is related to the attack ten years ago, and possibly to the missing girls." Another pause before Cash added, "Yes, sir. We'll give our statements once we're in a safe location." He handed her the phone. "Thanks."

"Is your boss upset?" She remembered Cash telling her he had come to Appleton despite his boss's opinion that he was on a wild-goose chase.

"Not anymore." The corner of Cash's mouth kicked up in a wry smile. "He actually said I was right to head up to talk to you."

"So he'll assign officers to keep us safe?"

The hint of a smile vanished. "No. To be honest, I'd rather we stay on our own."

"You don't think this guy is a cop, do you?"

"No, it's not that." Cash shook his head. "I trust my boss, but this guy knows my name, where I live. I can't risk the idea that he might glean some information from the police department. He could have a police scanner or some other way of getting intel. I'm not going to underestimate him again."

"Okay." She clearly wasn't about to argue. "Whatever you think is best."

Cash grimaced and gestured to the screen embedded in the dash. "Do me a favor and look up motels in Cross Plains."

She did as he asked, finding several options. "I didn't realize there was an Icelandic trail going through Cross Plains, Wisconsin."

He glanced at her. "I haven't been there, but I have heard about it. It's better if we head someplace neither of us has been before."

"I understand." She scanned the two motel options on the screen. "This motel looks like it's closer to the trail."

"That works." He changed lanes and took a ramp

leading west. She combed her fingers through her short, chin-length hair, feeling as if she'd run a marathon.

Escaping one relentless attack after another was wearing her down. The way this guy seemed to be a step ahead of them was not reassuring, either.

Somehow, she needed to make Cash understand it was time to switch from playing defense to going on the offense. And the best way to do that was to set a trap for this guy.

Setting her up someplace where he wouldn't be able to resist coming to grab her.

Her phone rang, startling her. Recognizing the number on the screen as Cash's lieutenant's, she handed it over.

"This is Rawson," Cash said curtly.

Jacy leaned forward, hoping to catch part of the conversation. As it turned out, the interaction between Cash and his boss was brief.

"Thanks. I'll be in touch." Cash handed back the phone. "The perp got away, but they're hopeful they'll get DNA evidence when they process the scene. They have already found three shell casings, which is a good start."

"I'm not surprised he got away." She remembered how he'd stood in the road, firing at them. "But where do you think he left his vehicle?"

"Good question." Cash scowled, his grip tightening on the steering wheel. She could tell he wanted to be back at the house, doing his part in collecting the evidence they'd need to find this guy. "I know the police will canvass the area, asking the neighbors what they heard and saw. I pray someone will have noticed a vehicle that seemed as if it didn't belong, giving us something concrete to go on."

She nodded, hoping they'd hear more positive news soon.

The trip to Cross Plains didn't take long. The town was more scenic than she'd anticipated; snow-covered trees dotted hills that were higher than the ravine she'd fallen down ten years ago.

It looked like a nice place to take a long hike, if it wasn't January. The peaceful scenery, though, was a balm to her nerves.

As if nothing bad could happen here.

Foolish thought, she silently chided. Bad things could and did happen anywhere. She was living proof of that. And so were the missing girls.

Cash pulled up to the motel then sat for a moment, staring blindly out the windshield. Finally, he asked, "Connecting rooms again?"

"Yes, please." She frowned. "Is something wrong?"

"Just wondering if this guy can track my credit card transactions." He pushed open the driver's-side door. "I'll use cash for tonight, but I will need to replenish my funds very soon."

"Okay." She didn't have a lot of cash in her bag but would gladly give every penny to Cash. No reason he should be paying for everything out of his own pocket.

While he was inside obtaining their rooms, she pulled out what she had. The measly fifty-three dollars she removed wouldn't take them very far. But it could cover the cost of gas and a fast-food meal.

Better than nothing.

Cash returned five minutes later. He slid into the driver's seat and handed her a key. "I'll need to park behind the building, I don't want this SUV visible from the road."

"Sure." She took the key and watched as he drove around to the far side of the motel. Cash grabbed their bags and the laptop case then walked to the side door.

Her key worked to access the building. Her room was right by the exit, with Cash's being one door down. Both overlooked the parking lot. Likely per Cash's request.

He dropped her bag on the bed while she unlocked the connecting door between their rooms. "How exactly are we going to work out providing a statement?"

"We're not doing that yet. I need to think about our next steps." He headed out the door, without giving her a chance to respond.

Biting back a wave of annoyance, she waited for him to open his side of their connecting rooms. When he did, she walked inside.

"I'm a part of this, Cash. We need to work together on our next steps." She crossed her arms over her chest. "I know I'm not a cop, but we need to figure out a way to draw this guy out."

"We're not using you as bait, Jacy." His sharp tone made her wince.

"Okay, but can't we set up a trap where it looks like I'm there? Even if I'm not?" She sat on the edge of the bed. "There must be something we can do."

Cash dragged his hand through his hair, his expression reflecting his frustration. "The one thing that would help the most is finding a hypnotist to work with you on remembering that night."

"Okay, I'm ready." She was willing to do whatever

he wanted. "Anything is better than sitting around and waiting for this guy to strike again."

Cash opened his laptop computer and powered it up. She watched over his shoulder as he searched for hypnosis services. Then he reached for his phone.

"Are you making an appointment?"

"No, I want to check with the department psychologist first." He gestured to the screen. "Dr. Shelly Abrams will know which of these people has a good reputation."

"Not Melanie, though," she reminded him.

"Got it." He listened for a moment then said, "I need to speak with Doctor Shelly Abrams."

Jacy stood and made her way back to her room. Now that the moment was upon her, she was oddly nervous. There had to be a way to break through the darkness surrounding the events from ten years ago.

She bowed her head, hoping and praying for the strength to withstand the revelations that were bound to emerge.

Please, Lord, I need Your strength and support to find the man responsible for hurting so many innocent women!

Cash noticed Jacy easing away, heading to her own room, and wondered if she was already second-guessing her agreement to be hypnotized.

As much as he didn't want to add to her anxiety, this was a necessary step if they were going to have any hope of finding this guy.

The shooting at his house had rattled him. Cash still wasn't sure why he'd chosen that moment to turn and get Jacy out of there, mere seconds before the gunfire erupted from his bedroom.

God had been watching over them today, that was for sure.

A voice on the other end of the line interrupted his thoughts. "I'm sorry, Detective Rawson, but Doctor Abrams is in a meeting with the assistant chief. I'll have her call you back when she's finished, shouldn't be long."

"Okay, thank you." Cash rattled off his new number and disconnected the call. Sitting back in his chair, he scrubbed his hands over his face.

This was the first time the perp had responded with a high level of violence. Sure, pepper spray, a smoke bomb and a dart gun were all forms of violence, but the gunfire the perp had leveled at them today? Any one of those bullets could have hit Jacy in the head or the heart. Proof, in his opinion, that this guy was beyond just trying to get his hands on her.

No, it was clear this guy's intent was to kill them both, eliminating them as a potential threat.

Permanently.

When had his goal changed? Cash wondered. Was it because they'd kept managing to escape the previous attacks? Or had it been the way Cash had fired his weapon at the perp when he'd used the tranquilizer gun at the ridge?

He nodded to himself. Yeah, this guy was becoming desperate. That was good and bad. Desperate people often made mistakes.

But a desperate man was also twice as dangerous.

"When do we leave?"

Jacy's question had him turning to face her. "The doc was in a meeting. I'm waiting to hear back."

"Okay." Was it his imagination or was there a hint of relief in her eyes? "Here, this is all the cash I have. I figure you should use it for gas and food as needed."

He reluctantly took the money from her. He didn't like being in this position, but his decision to go to his place hadn't worked out so well. And his own reserves were running low. "Thanks, Jacy."

"I—uh, we should think about lunch." She glanced out the window at the beautiful view of snow-covered evergreen trees. "I didn't see anything within walking distance, though."

"Yeah." He couldn't muster much enthusiasm for the idea. If he had his way, Jacy would stay hidden in the motel with a dozen armed guards until they had this perp behind bars.

Was he wrong not to ask for additional backup from the Madison PD? No way would Timmons provide even a couple of cops to use as backup; their budget would never support that. But his boss might free up one officer to help guard Jacy.

"Cash?" Jacy tipped her head to the side. "What are you thinking?"

"Nothing for you to worry about." He shook off his troubling thoughts. Right now, no one knew where they were. There was no electronic trail to lead anyone to this motel in Cross Plains. "Lunch sounds good. Hopefully we'll hear back from Doctor Abrams by then."

"Great." Her smile didn't quite reach her eyes. "I'll be glad to get that over with."

He rose to his feet and reached for his coat. "I remember seeing a small diner not far from here. I need a few minutes, though, before we leave."

"To do what?"

He ducked into the bathroom, emerging with a glass of warm water. "I'm going to make mud to cover the license plate. Just as a precaution, since the shooter did come out onto the street as we were driving away."

"I'm sure he didn't get the number," she protested. "We were going fast, and he was too busy shooting to memorize it."

"Maybe, but I'm not taking any more chances. Wait here."

He turned and headed outside. One advantage to parking along the back of the building was that there wouldn't be anyone to watch as he poured the warm water on the frozen ground to make mud. He didn't obliterate the entire license plate as that might be suspicious, but he did the middle section, spreading enough mud to other areas of the plate, too, to make it look natural.

Satisfied, he headed back into the motel to clean up. He was surprised to find Jacy at his computer. After washing up in the bathroom, he joined her.

"Maybe we don't need to wait to hear from your doc." She tapped the screen. "Looks like there are several hypnotist options, all back in Madison, though. I think it might be better to just pick the one that has time to see us today."

"You're really determined to do this?"

"I am." She stared at the computer for a long moment. "I want this over, Cash. I want to find the person responsible, and to see if these young women are still alive."

"I want that, too," he murmured, lightly squeezing

her shoulder. "Okay, we'll bring the computer with us. If we haven't heard from Abrams by the time we're finished eating, we'll start making calls."

"Good." She closed the laptop and stood. "That's good."

Was she trying to convince him? Or herself?

A few minutes later, they were back on the road, cruising the small quaint town of Cross Plains. Under different circumstances, he'd be thrilled to spend more time here, hiking the Icelandic trail.

But right now, he was too focused on searching the cars around him for a potential threat.

Thankfully, he didn't see anyone resembling the assailant. One thing that worked to their advantage was that this guy continued to hide his face. It made Cash think the culprit was concerned that if he simply approached them without a mask, Jacy would recognize him.

The diner wasn't too crowded. They easily found a booth next to the window. It was cold there, though, and he noticed Jacy kept her coat on.

"We can take an order to go, if you'd rather eat at the motel," he offered.

"No, this is fine," she assured him.

They placed their order. Their server brought coffee, too. Jacy's eyes lit up as she cradled the cup in her hands.

He was glad for the kick of caffeine after the rush of adrenaline had faded. When their food arrived, Jacy set down her coffee and reached for his hand. "I'd like to say grace."

"Of course." He hid his surprise.

"Dear Lord Jesus, thank You for keeping us safe,

today. We are also thankful for this food You have provided for us. Help me to be strong as I seek answers from the past. Amen."

"Amen." Her prayer was humbling. "You're going to do fine, Jacy."

"I hope so."

They were halfway through the meal before his phone rang. Recognizing Dr. Shelly Abrams's number, he quickly answered.

"Detective Rawson."

"Detective, this is Shelly. I understand you're looking for a hypnotist for a witness."

He met Jacy's eyes. "I am, yes. Jacy Urban was attacked ten years ago, but fell down into a ravine and has no memory of her assailant."

"I remember that case very well. Head injuries that result in memory loss can be tricky," Abrams said. "Hypnosis doesn't always work in those situations. I'd like to meet with Jacy, see if I can help."

"You would?" He had trouble hiding his shock. "I didn't realize you did hypnosis."

"I trained a few years ago, yes. When and where would you like to meet? I'm open the rest of the afternoon."

"Any chance you can meet us in Cross Plains?" He rattled off the address of their motel. "I think it's best if we stay away from Madison for a while."

"That's fine. I'll meet you there in a half hour."

"Thanks, Doc." He lowered his phone. "Dr. Abrams is going to do the hypnosis herself."

"Okay." She stared down at her half-eaten meal then looked up at him. "I promise to do my best."

"That's all I ask." He reached over to take her hand. Her fingers were ice cold.

And he could tell that, despite this being her idea, Jacy was scared to death of what she was about to remember.

TEN

Swallowing hard against the ball of fear lodged in her throat, Jacy tried to shake off the sense of foreboding. Being hypnotized was what she wanted. She desperately needed to remember who had assaulted her so Cash and the other police officers could put him behind bars.

For the rest of his miserable life.

She toyed with her french fry, trying to settle her stomach. She didn't want to waste food, not when they were low on finances, but she wasn't sure she could finish her turkey wrap.

"Would you like dessert?" their server asked, eyeing the remains of Jacy's meal with an arched eyebrow. "We have peach pie."

"No, thanks, but may I please have a to-go box?" Jacy gestured to her food. Cold fries were not nearly as appetizing as cold pizza, but she would not let them go to waste. Especially not when they were low on cash.

"Sure, hon." The woman returned a few minutes later with the box and their bill. "Have a nice day."

"You, too," Cash said, pulling money from his pocket while Jacy put her leftovers in the cardboard container. Then he glanced at her. "Don't be nervous. Doctor Abrams is great. She'll do her best to make you comfortable."

"I'm sure she will." She wasn't nervous, but apprehensive. That wasn't logical as memories couldn't hurt her. Not the way bullets could.

She reminded herself that if this hypnosis was successful, it was entirely possible that the assailant would be behind bars before the end of the day.

"Ready to head back?" Cash asked.

"Yes." She injected confidence in her tone. "Let's do this."

"That's my girl," he said, sliding out of the booth.

His girl? The words warmed her heart, even though she knew they weren't true. Although their brief kiss had left her wanting more, she'd been the one to instigate the embrace, not him. She picked up her leftovers, while Cash caught her hand in his as they made their way out to the SUV.

Cash's eyes swept the area. He unlocked the SUV, releasing her so he could open the passenger door. His protective attitude was sweet, but probably unnecessary here in Cross Plains.

Her phone rang on the way back to the motel. Recognizing the lieutenant's number, she handed the phone to Cash.

This time, she could hear the other side of the conversation because Lieutenant Timmons yelled, "Where are you? I thought you were coming in to give your statement!"

Cash didn't look fazed. "We have a few things to do first. Besides, I told you we'd give our statements over the phone. I don't want to take Jacy back to Madison."

"Leaving the city wasn't part of the plan!" Timmons shouted.

"I understand, sir, but keeping Jacy safe is my primary objective." Cash paused then told him, "We're on the road. I'll call you once we're settled."

There was a long pause where Jacy imagined Lieutenant Timmons was wrestling his temper under control. "Fine. Call me back ASAP."

"Yes, sir." Cash handed the phone to her.

"He sounded really mad."

Cash shrugged. "He'll get over it. He knows that keeping you safe is important. He's just angry I didn't clear it with him first."

"Don't put your job on the line for me."

"He won't fire me over this." Cash offered a lopsided grin. "He might write me up for insubordination, but he won't fire me."

"That's not much better." She couldn't hide her exasperation.

"It's more important to keep you safe." He lifted a hand, as if sensing her protest. "Don't worry, Jacy. We'll give our statements over the phone soon enough."

She let it go, sensing more arguing would be futile. He could be incredibly stubborn.

A trait that was far more annoying than endearing.

When they reached the motel, Cash drove around back, the same way he had before. They went in through the side door. Glancing at the clock on the nightstand after storing her leftovers in the small fridge, Jacy's stomach tightened as she realized Dr. Shelly Abrams would be there in twenty minutes.

Sitting still was impossible, so she paced the room. This would work. This had to work.

At least two young girls' lives depended on it.

"Jacy?" Cash stepped through the connecting door. "Where would you be more comfortable? Your room or mine?"

"Doesn't matter." She did her best to smile reassuringly. "One motel room is much like another."

"Where did you get hypnotized the first time?"

"In the psychologist's office." She glanced around the room. "It was darker than this. I hope that isn't a problem."

"We can ask the doc, but I'm sure it will be fine." He took a step toward her. "I want you to know that, no matter how this turns out, I'm impressed by your courage."

That was an outright exaggeration. Real courage was protecting her while bullets were flying, but she didn't voice her thought. Cash was being his usual nice and supportive self. His intent was to put her at ease.

Too bad, it didn't work.

"I'd like to call Timmons to provide our statements," Cash continued. "We should be able to do that before Doctor Abrams arrives."

"Sure. That's fine." Anything to keep her mind off the hypnosis session looming over her.

Despite her concern over Cash's job, his boss had calmed down enough to listen as they provided their statements related to the gunfire at Cash's house. The process took longer than she'd expected, mostly because Lieutenant Timmons and the officer with him kept asking questions.

"The bedroom door being closed was a signal that someone had been inside," Cash said. "I can say with certainty that if I hadn't followed my gut instincts to get Jacy out of there, we'd both be injured, or possibly dead."

"I thought this guy was trying to take her alive?" Timmons asked.

"That's what I thought, too. He's either getting impatient or knew that I'd protect Jacy with my own life. Maybe he assumed she'd be okay."

"Humph." Timmons didn't sound like he agreed.

"Anything else?" Cash asked, his stare focused on the window overlooking the parking lot.

"No, that's all for now," Timmons grudgingly said. "But I expect you to keep me in the loop, Rawson. No more changing the plan at the last minute."

"I will. Later." Cash punched the end button on the phone. "Looks like the doc is here."

"I see that." Her stomach knotted as they both watched the woman approach the motel.

Dr. Shelly Abrams appeared to be in her early forties, with long dark hair pulled back from her face in a bun. She greeted Jacy warmly.

"It's good to meet you, Jacy." Her eyes were full of compassion.

"You, too." Jacy tried to shake off the lingering apprehension. "Should we get started?"

"Let's chat for a few minutes first." Dr. Abrams sat in the chair near the bed. "I know you tried this before."

"Yes." Jacy gave her a brief rundown on her previous and unsuccessful attempts to remember the past. "I'm hoping I'm stronger and wiser now."

"Head injuries can be tricky," Shelly said, her regard sympathetic. "So if this doesn't work, I don't want you to think it's all your fault."

She relaxed a bit at that. For years, she'd assumed

she was immune to hypnosis. That somehow she'd purposefully resisted it. But maybe it was just that getting bonked on the head had caused the deep abyss in her memory.

After a few minutes, Shelly asked her to stretch out on the bed. Jacy was conscious of Cash hovering in the doorway between their rooms.

The doc spoke in low soothing tones, asking her to relax and to concentrate on a specific memory. "Hold that image in your mind," Shelly said.

The image was a crystal necklace that her mother had given her for her sixteenth birthday. Jacy had been wearing it the day she'd been abducted and had worn it almost every day since. Reaching up, she clasped the crystal in her hand.

Shelly continued to talk to her, asking her to return to the day she'd been walking home from choir practice. Jacy closed her eyes and did her best to relax and to go back in time. She saw the Colgate house clearly enough.

Yet, no matter how many times Shelly asked her to remember who had called out to her on the sidewalk that day—information Cash had obviously provided to help facilitate the process—there was still a black void where her memory should be.

"I'm sorry, it's just not working." Jacy let go of the crystal necklace and swung up into a sitting position. She avoided Cash's gaze, not wanting to see the keen disappointment in his eyes. "I told you I'm immune to hypnosis."

"Your subconscious is definitely resisting the process," Shelly agreed. The doc eyed her curiously. "Your head injury might be part of the problem. I've never had a patient resist hypnosis like this without some additional factor influencing the outcome."

Was that supposed to make her feel better? Yeah, it didn't.

Worse, they were no closer to finding the assailant or the missing teenage girls.

Cash pushed aside the disappointment at the lack of progress. He walked Dr. Abrams outside. "What do you think, Doc? Is she resisting on purpose? Or is this really because of her head injury?"

Shelly shrugged. "Honestly, both. I watched the way she held the crystal pendant. Her fingers never fully relaxed. I tried to give her ample time to let go of her fears, but I don't think she did. And maybe, she really can't remember." Shelly grimaced as she met his eyes. "It's possible she never will remember. Even if or when she sees the assailant again."

That possibility concerned him. He nodded slowly. "Okay, thanks. I really appreciate you giving this a try."

"Not getting through is a first for me, and I'd like to try again, maybe in a different setting."

Cash wasn't at all convinced Jacy would want to repeat the experience. "We'll keep that in mind. For now, we'll have to continue working the case by digging up clues and following where they might lead."

"Understood." Shelly opened her car door and slid inside. "If Jacy does make a breakthrough at some point, I'd like to hear about it. Maybe then we'll understand why our session didn't work."

"Will do." He straightened, watching as Shelly backed out of the parking space and drove away.

As always, he scanned the area before turning to

head inside. There were fewer cars out front now than there had been earlier. He assumed people had checked out and that more would be arriving later in the day.

He'd feel better if the place was deserted, except for the two of them, but that wasn't practical. If he had unlimited funds, he could rent all the rooms, but that was impossible.

Truth was, he'd need to stop at an ATM the following day for more cash. It seemed impossible that this perp could be tracking his credit card or ATM withdrawals, but he wasn't about to take any unnecessary chances.

He found Jacy waiting for him in his room. "I'm sorry I couldn't help…" she began.

"Jacy, I told you before, all I asked is that you would try." He stepped closer, putting his arm around her shoulders. "We'll keep at it. Something will break soon."

"I hope so," she whispered, sounding totally dejected. "I really tried to relax. But I couldn't. Not even when I focused on my crystal necklace."

He tipped his head to the side. "Did you use the crystal necklace as a focal point in your first session ten years ago?"

"Yes." She frowned. "Why wouldn't I? It was a gift from my parents. It's the only jewelry I wear."

"And you were wearing it the night of the abduction?" Cash said.

"Yes, but why would that matter? Doctor Abrams said it was just a talisman of sorts to help relax."

He found that curious but figured there was no point in pushing the issue, so he let it go. "Why don't you try to get some rest?"

"While you do what?" Jacy asked.

"Earlier, I discovered there's a site where you can find old yearbooks that have been scanned in online." It was a far better option than buying one directly from a former student. Maybe he was being overly cautious, but he wasn't quite ready to head back to the city.

Not until this perp had been tossed behind bars.

"I'll help." Jacy crossed her arms at her chest. "After all, I'm the one who needs to look at the various photos, anyway."

Since she was right, he simply nodded. The computer was in his room, so she brought her chair over to crowd next to him.

He found the yearbook site and quickly located the one for the year Jacy was a sophomore in high school. He was surprised they were so readily available, but relieved, too. At least this way, they could review the pictures from the safety of the motel.

"Wow, it's weird going back in time," Jacy murmured as he clicked on the yearbook. The first few pages were candid shots of students involved in various activities.

"Is there a place where they list the teachers?" Jacy asked. "That may be a place to start."

It was a good idea, so he quickly paged through the book, searching for teacher photos. There were many photos to wade through, and he noticed there were a few group photos of the choir. He made a mental note to return to those for a closer look, but had to go through the entire yearbook just to discover there were no pictures of the teachers.

"Figures," Jacy said on a sigh. "If we go back to the

theory of a substitute teacher being involved, this review of photographs won't help."

"I know, but look at it this way." He turned a bit in his seat to face her. "We need to cross off the possibility of a fellow student being the perp."

"I guess. I still think I'd remember if the assailant was a classmate." She gestured to the screen. "We can go through the list of all the sophomores. That may be a place to start."

He considered mentioning the choir group photo but thought she might be right about going through her classmates first. He turned the computer so that it was facing her.

She spent a lot of time looking intently at one photo before moving on to the next. The scent of her shampoo wafted toward him, oddly reminding him of their kiss.

He forced himself not to think about pulling Jacy into his arms again. Finding the perp responsible for these attacks was the only goal.

Not looking for an excuse to kiss her again.

She was on the second page when he noticed movement out the window. Easing back away from the small table, he edged closer to see who was out there.

A black truck with tinted windows pulled up in front of the motel lobby. Cash found himself holding his breath as he waited for the driver to emerge from the vehicle.

Only, he never did. After a long moment, the truck backed up and roared away. Cash narrowed his eyes on the license plate, but there wasn't one. At the last minute, before the truck disappeared around the corner, he noticed a temporary plate propped in the rear window above the truck bed.

The tiny hairs on the back of his neck lifted in warning. Logically, he knew people bought replacement vehicles all the time. But why had the truck pulled in, only to leave just as abruptly a few minutes later?

Was he making a big deal out of nothing? Maybe, but Cash still didn't like it. It didn't seem possible that the assailant could have found their hiding spot.

Then again, he had asked Dr. Shelly Abrams to come out to meet with them. He didn't think that was a call that had gone through the police radio, unless Shelly had updated his boss about the lack of progress with the procedure? Maybe.

The unease in his gut wouldn't leave him alone. Remembering how he'd turned from his bedroom in the nick of time, he decided this wasn't the moment to ignore his instincts.

"Jacy, we need to get out of here. Now." He turned from the window, pulling the computer away. "We'll look at the photos later. Get your stuff."

"Why? What's happening?"

"Just get your things." He shoved the laptop into the bag as he spoke. "Hurry!"

Jacy jumped up and ran into the connecting room. Seconds later, she emerged, carrying her bag. "I'm ready."

"Good. Stay behind me," he warned as they left their rooms. The narrow hallway was empty. He rushed to the end of the hall to peer out the door.

Seeing nothing alarming, he pushed through. Thankfully, Jacy stayed right behind him, holding on to his jacket as they moved as one to the SUV.

He was glad he'd parked in the back of the building, and that he'd taken time to muddy the license plate. He quickly tossed their bags in the rear, while Jacy climbed into the passenger seat.

After settling behind the wheel, he started the SUV and moved forward. Just as the black truck with the tinted windows returned.

"Get down," he shouted, hitting the gas.

The SUV surged forward. He yanked hard on the steering wheel, to drive around the truck. Thankfully, he had plenty of open road ahead of him to work with. Tires squealed from behind him as the truck attempted to turn around.

No! He couldn't let this guy get to them!

Cash jammed his foot on the gas pedal, pressing it almost all the way to the floor. The SUV sped down the road, eating up the miles. He alternated between watching the speedometer go higher and higher, and the rearview mirror.

They were far enough ahead now that he couldn't see the truck behind them. But he wouldn't relax. Not yet.

Cash was forced to slow down for the upcoming curve in the road. He glanced around, trying to figure out where to go next.

"Cash? The truck is back!" Jacy cried.

Sure enough, a quick glance in the rearview mirror indicated the truck was gaining on them.

Tightening his grip on the steering wheel, Cash hit the gas hard, praying the engine of this SUV would have the power they needed to avoid being caught by the big imposing truck.

He couldn't let this guy catch up to them.

ELEVEN

The black truck was gaining on them! Jacy gripped the door handle tightly. Cash was driving incredibly fast for these winding country roads.

Not that he had much of a choice.

Remembering how they'd rolled over across the field when the brake line had been tampered with had her imagining the same fate today. Only this time, there was a chance they wouldn't walk away. Especially if they were struck by the truck.

Another car headed toward them from the opposite direction. Jacy held her breath. Their tires squealed as Cash took the curve around the car.

"Hang on," he encouraged as they approached an intersection. He hit the brakes hard to make a right-hand turn then punched the accelerator again. She realized he had the map app up on his dashboard screen. Thankfully, there was another intersection a few miles away.

This time, Cash turned left. "Call 9-1-1 and report the black Ford truck with tinted windows."

"But—we don't have a license plate." She let go of the door handle to reach for the phone.

"Just tell them about the lack of front plates and

only a temporary plate in the back window. Let the dispatcher know the truck was last seen on Highway 15, heading out of Cross Plains."

"Okay." She made the call, striving to sound confident as she relayed the message. They were heading farther away from Madison, making her wonder how long it would take for a law enforcement response.

Too long, she thought in despair.

Cash slowed the SUV and then surprised her by pulling over.

"What are you doing?"

He didn't answer right away, but his intent became clear as he drove off the road and into the wooded area. Then he backed up, so that their vehicle was hidden between a pair of bushy pine trees.

"Sit tight." He pushed out of the SUV and crossed over to pull branches from the tree, strategically placing them around the SUV. Then he used another pine tree branch to cover their tire tracks. The snow was spotty on the ground anyway, thanks to the milder than normal temps, which helped. When he was finished, she couldn't tell a car had driven into the woods.

After what seemed like eons, Cash eased back behind the wheel.

"Now what? We're just going to wait and see if the truck passes by?" She shivered at the thought of the driver noticing them and coming after them. He'd used a gun back at Cash's house.

She thought it highly likely he still had the weapon. Not to mention, the tranquilizer gun, too. She trusted Cash's cop instincts yet couldn't help feeling a bit vulnerable out here in the woods.

And maybe that was the point. The guy driving

the truck wouldn't think they'd hide in the woods. He would assume they'd head to the next closest town.

"Too bad we don't have binoculars," he muttered. "But, yes, we're going to sit here for a while. I want this perp to believe he's lost us."

"What if he already thinks he's lost us?" She glanced at Cash. "He may never head down this road."

"He might not," Cash agreed. "Especially if the cops patrolling the area find him."

She wanted to ask how long they'd have to sit in the cold but held her tongue. Cash couldn't predict the future. They'd just have to wait and see what happened.

The minutes ticked by slowly. She'd enjoyed the heated seats, but now the warmth was fading and a deep chill was settling in her bones. The weather might be mild for January, but it was still freezing.

Gritting her teeth, she told herself not to complain. Cash was doing his best to keep them safe.

"Can you hold out a little longer?" The way he seemed to know exactly what she was thinking unnerved her.

"Yes." She softly gasped. "Cash! Is that the truck?"

As if on cue, a large black truck with tinted windows rolled past. It wasn't going nearly as fast now.

"Yep, that's it." Cash's gaze tracked the vehicle until it was out of sight. "The good news is that he didn't notice us here."

"What's the bad news?"

He grinned wryly. "We need to stay put for a while longer in case he doubles back this way."

"That's fine." She tried not to shiver.

He reached over to take her hand. "I can start the car for a few minutes."

Tempting, but she shook her head. "No need. I wouldn't want to give away our location."

"Me, either. But I think he'll follow this road for a while yet."

Clinging to Cash's hand, she found strength in his touch. On some level, she knew Cash wasn't anything like Greg Archer, the Appleton cop she'd once dated. But at the same time, she knew this was a temporary interlude. Nothing that would last forever.

She liked her life the way it was. Uncomplicated and unencumbered. Greg had gotten annoyed when she'd been called out to do sketches at odd hours, or on the weekends he had off.

Glancing at Cash, she couldn't imagine him being annoyed at her being called out to sketch a suspect. Too bad he lived and worked in Madison.

And she had no desire to go back to the city where she'd been a victim. Madison was part of her past. Appleton, and the surrounding police departments she worked with, were her future. A future she couldn't enjoy until this assailant was caught and placed behind bars.

"You need to set me up as bait to draw this guy out."

"No. We had this discussion, remember?" Cash sounded annoyed.

"Yet here we are, hiding in the woods because he keeps finding us," she shot back.

"He must have followed Abrams, or learned she'd come to the motel where we were staying," Cash said grimly. "I don't know how, maybe someone used the radio to ask about meeting with her, only to be told she was at our motel. It's the only thing that makes sense."

"Could be that he has connections within the Madison Police Department. Which will work in our favor to set a trap for him."

"Then who am I going to trust to act as backup?" Cash asked harshly. "Not anyone within the Madison PD."

"Detective Vargas, for one." She thought for a moment. "Although, I have to admit, the two missing girls in Appleton could mean this guy is now working locally."

"As a cop?" Cash twisted in his seat. Their breathing was causing the windows to fog up, so he turned on the engine long enough to defog them. "How would that even be possible?"

"I don't know." She shook her head. "I figured he'd been arrested at some point, otherwise I feel like he'd have left a trail of missing blonde girls in his wake."

"I had the same thought." Cash hesitated for a moment. "I don't see this perp as a cop. The recent assaults don't come across as being done by a professional. I'm leaning toward the substitute teacher angle."

"Maybe, but I don't remember a substitute teacher at the high school." She wished she did; it would be easy enough to follow up to see if that same teacher had worked elsewhere.

"What about a long-term substitute?" Cash asked.

"I don't remember one." Then she frowned. "To be honest, if one of my teachers was a long-term sub, I'm not sure we as students would know. Especially if the teacher started at the beginning of the school year. The other students and I went from class to class without really knowing much about a teacher's background."

"Keep thinking on it," Cash said. "Maybe something will come to you."

"Don't hold your breath," she muttered. It burned to know her attempt to be hypnotized had failed. "My mind has done nothing but let me down."

"Or it's protecting you, Jacy. Try not to think the worst, okay?"

She wanted to go back to setting a trap, but at that moment the sound of an engine reached their ears. She could hear the truck before it rolled by.

The same black truck, with the same tinted windows. Jacy held her breath, as this time, the Ford was moving more slowly, as if sensing they were hiding in the woods, watching.

Cash's fingers tightened on hers. She understood he was signaling her to remain silent. Not a problem, as she couldn't have spoken if she'd wanted to.

After the truck disappeared down the street, they continued waiting for several long minutes.

Finally, she broke the silence. "Don't you see, Cash? He's never going to stop looking for us. Setting a trap for him is the only option."

"I can agree that he'll keep looking." Cash didn't move, his contemplation still on the windshield. "I just wish I knew who to trust."

"Call Detective Vargas," she urged. "He'll help us set a trap for this guy. Heading back to Appleton is probably the best idea, anyway." She couldn't deny a deep desire to get far away from Madison.

Enough was enough. Trying to spur her blocked memories had only resulted in several attempts to kill them.

And she was very much afraid if they didn't try something different, the man in the black truck would succeed in his mission.

* * *

Cash ground his molars together. If Jacy mentioned setting herself up as bait one more time, he was going to lose it.

What part of not an option didn't she understand? He was beyond annoyed at the way she kept bringing the subject up. As if her stubborn persistence was going to change his mind.

When she began to shiver, he started the engine again. He wasn't ready to leave the sanctuary of the woods yet but didn't want to see her suffer, either.

On the heels of that realization came another. If Jacy was anyone else, would he agree to set her up as bait?

No, of course not. The police did not use innocent victims like that.

Except, of course, they sometimes did. Especially when there was no alternative.

Fine, then he'd have to find a different approach. Because he couldn't bring himself to use Jacy in that way.

Not even to save another innocent teenage girl? He winced at the question that flashed in the back of his mind. And knew the answer was a resounding no. Not even then.

"Thanks, I'm warmer now," Jacy said, breaking the strained silence.

"I don't want to leave until we know for sure the truck won't return." They'd been sitting there for thirty minutes already. The truck had returned after twenty minutes, so he wanted to wait at least that much longer.

Maybe more.

Over the next few minutes, he ran the engine until the seats had warmed up. Then he shut down again, unwilling to disclose their location.

"Can I grab my sketchbook?" Jacy asked.

"Sure, I'll get it for you." He was glad for an excuse to get out of the vehicle. After he pulled her sketchbook and pencils from her bag and handed them to her, he decided to walk along the tree line. "I'll be back in a few minutes."

"Okay." Jacy was already starting to sketch their surroundings.

He thought again about how good she was at her job, and wondered why this perp had decided to come after her all these years later.

On some level, it didn't make sense. Since Jacy hadn't sketched his likeness and put it out there for law enforcement officers to use.

Unless, of course, this guy was obsessed with her as the one who'd gotten away.

He moved along the woods, keeping a keen eye on the highway. Another vehicle appeared on the horizon, but it was a small, bright blue, two-door sedan that whizzed past.

Not the perp.

He stood for a moment, scanning the landscape. He was tempted to get out of there, but knew it would be better to wait.

Making his way back to the SUV, he tried to come up with a plan to use a female police officer who resembled Jacy enough that they might be able to draw this guy out of hiding. Because Jacy was right about one thing.

This running and hiding from the assailant was getting old.

He slid behind the wheel, glancing over at Jacy's sketch, somewhat disappointed it wasn't his likeness.

Pushing the ridiculous thought away, he said, "I didn't realize you drew landscapes."

"I draw everything," she said with a grin. "But getting details from witnesses to draw suspects is my best skill."

He couldn't deny that. Gesturing to the portfolio, he asked, "Can I see them?"

"Sure." She continued drawing as if she wasn't paying him much attention.

As he reached for the portfolio, his phone rang. Startled, he dropped the portfolio and grabbed the device. It took a moment for him to recognize Detective Vargas's number.

"Detective Rawson," he answered.

"It's Vargas. Is Jacy with you?"

"Yes. Do you want me to place the call on speaker?"

"No, hearing this news might upset her. A dog found the remains of a young teenage girl half buried beneath rocks under a railroad bridge. I'm heading there now to see if the body might be one of our missing girls, either Claire or Suzanna."

He winced, knowing Vargas was right. The news that the missing girl might be dead would be devastating. "Where are you? I'd like to see the area."

Jacy sucked in a harsh breath. "Which girl is it?"

"We don't know yet," he said to Jacy. Then into the phone, added, "Vargas? I know we're a couple of hours away, but we're heading north now." He started the engine on the SUV.

"Actually, the body was found halfway between Appleton and Madison," Vargas said. "Outside a small town called Bakersville."

"Bakersville?" Cash repeated, pulling out from their

hiding spot. The branches fell away as he led the SUV over the rocky terrain. "Do you think that location is significant?"

"Not sure," Vargas said. "The place is barely a dot on the map. I'm heading there now."

"See you soon then." Cash set the phone aside. Once they reached the road, he keyed up the map on the dashboard screen. Following the directions, they'd get to Bakersville in an hour and fifteen minutes.

Faster, if he pushed the speed limit, which he fully intended to do.

"They're dead, aren't they?" Jacy whispered. She'd set her sketchbook aside. "All of the missing girls are dead."

"We don't know that. Let's not jump to conclusions." He tried to sound confident, but deep down, he'd always suspected the missing girls had been killed.

And if Bakersville was the dump site? The town had to have some sort of significance for their perp.

"I should have died that night," Jacy said. "Maybe if I hadn't escaped, this guy wouldn't have grabbed the other innocent girls."

"Jacy, please don't torture yourself over this." He wanted to reach over to take her hand, but he was pushing the speed limit and needed both hands on the wheel. "There's only one man who is responsible for this. Not you."

She didn't answer, but stared out the windshield. Between making sure they didn't run across the black truck, and getting to Bakersville as quickly as possible, he had to concentrate on the road.

Even though he'd rather offer Jacy some comfort.

"Help me watch for the black Ford truck," he finally said. "Let me know if you see it."

"I will."

They didn't talk much as he navigated the traffic around Madison. Once he'd passed the big city, he was able to push the speed limit further.

In the end, they made good time in reaching Bakersville. Vargas was right about the town being barely a blip on the map. It was so small, Cash thought he'd have missed it completely if he hadn't been looking for it.

Finding the cluster of police vehicles off to the side of the road wasn't difficult since there was hardly any traffic at all in the area. There weren't any houses in the immediate vicinity that he could see. Almost fifty yards from the road, there was a creek, with a railroad bridge reaching from one side to the other with high iron arches. It was hard to tell if the tracks were still in use.

Strange for their perp to have hidden the body here.

Maybe the dead girl was someone else. Obviously, a dead girl was always terrible, no matter who she was, but he found himself hoping the young teenage girl wasn't Suzanna Perry or Claire Simmons.

As he and Jacy got out of the SUV, he saw Detective Vargas standing down at the creek bank, near the base of the bridge. He and several officers had circled around a pile of rocks.

"Jacy, stay here. You don't need to see this."

"Yes, I do." She looked pale but determined. "I'm coming with you."

He held out his hand and she took it. Together they went down the embankment to approach the scene. The ground was hard and icy beneath their feet, and the water in the creek was frozen. The temp was a little colder here than in Madison.

"He used the rocks to try to bury the body," Vargas said by way of greeting. "I'm sure the killer figured no one would search here, but thankfully a marathon runner was going past and his dog found it."

Cash braced himself. This wouldn't be the first dead body he'd seen, but he knew it was likely Jacy's. He wished she'd have stayed back, but she stood stoically beside him, gazing down at the girl who was still partially covered with rocks.

"She looks like Suzanna Perry," Jacy whispered.

Cash silently agreed. He met Vargas's gaze, arching a brow. The detective nodded.

"She's wearing the same clothing that Suzanna had on the day she disappeared," Vargas said. "We'll need her parents to make a firm ID, but I believe it's her."

"Where's her necklace?" Jacy stepped closer, a crease furrowing her brow. "I thought the picture showed her wearing a moon-shaped necklace."

"No sign of it. And no sign of her winter coat, either." Vargas grimaced and Cash knew exactly what he was thinking.

The killer had kept the necklace and maybe even the coat as souvenirs.

It made him realize this guy was a serial killer, one who likely wouldn't stop.

Until they caught him.

TWELVE

It took all of Jacy's willpower not to throw up on the crime scene. Or to fall apart, crumpling to the ground in a heap. Cash wouldn't appreciate that, especially as she had insisted on coming along.

Yet she turned away, pulling from his grasp. This was worse than she'd imagined, and it gave her some inkling as to what he and the other detectives dealt with every day.

Taking a few steps back, she drew in a few shallow breaths. The news of Suzanna Perry's death wasn't that surprising. Deep down, she'd always suspected the two missing girls wouldn't be found alive.

But seeing the results of this killer's despicable work was devastating. No young girl should end up in a shallow grave, covered with loose rocks near a frozen creek and mostly hidden beneath a railroad bridge. She doubted the killer had expected the body to be uncovered by a marathon runner and his dog.

Even from her stance at the edge of the gravesite, she could see the dark bruises that had encircled Suzanna's neck. Jacy was no expert but had to believe Suzanna had been strangled to death.

She lifted her hand to her throat, unable to imagine how the poor girl had suffered.

Behind her, she could hear Vargas and Cash speaking in low tones. She continued walking back up the embankment toward the SUV parked along the side of the road. Soon, the voices faded, leaving only silence in her wake.

Suzanna's missing necklace niggled at the back of her mind, making her reach up to touch the crystal around her neck.

Would the killer have taken her necklace, too, if he'd succeeded in holding her hostage ten years ago? She tried to think back to the picture she'd seen of Claire Simmons. There wasn't a necklace in the photo that she remembered. But the young girl had been wearing blue earrings, and possibly rings on her fingers, too.

She told herself the jewelry didn't matter, at least not at this point. Maybe it was something that would help down the road.

But first, they had to find him.

Walking a few feet, she stood gazing out at the sleepy landscape. The lack of activity in the area must have been a factor in the killer's deciding to bury Suzanna's body here. Had he known this area? That the creek would have rocks to use to cover Suzanna's body? Both girls had disappeared in winter, which would have made disposing of their bodies difficult.

Had he left Claire's body nearby, too?

Hunching her shoulders against the cool breeze, she took in another shaky breath. If both Suzanna and Claire were dead, she felt certain the three girls—Emily, Beth and Kim—had likely suffered the same fate.

Five young women were dead. *Dead!* All because of

her? No, she couldn't handle that. Cash seemed to think this guy would have kept killing, regardless of her escape, but what if he was wrong? She never wanted to believe this was personal, but the connection of every missing girl being in high school made her think it was.

That, and how they all looked similar to the way she had ten years ago.

Maybe she needed to think more about every guy she'd turned down for a date. As insane as it sounded, her rejection may have been enough to send this person off the deep end. Yet even as the thought entered her mind, she couldn't fathom it. For one thing, she was hardly a guy magnet. During her sophomore year, there was only one boy she'd turned down for a date, and Jacob Harding had ended up seeing one of her classmates, Julie, on a regular basis after that. It didn't make sense that he would have cared enough about her rejection to do something as awful as this.

In truth, she couldn't recall anyone asking her out and being upset about her declining his offer. She'd had more guys who were simply good friends, rather than guys who were interested in being her boyfriend. She began culling her memory for boys in her circle.

Both Robbie White and James Carmichael had been good friends of hers.

She'd dated Steve Crane for a few months, but even that relationship had simply fizzled out, without any drama or fanfare. They'd both been busy in their respective lives with after-school activities and hadn't cared enough about each other to keep things going. No reason for Steve to have gotten upset over it.

Massaging her temple, Jacy trudged along the side of the road, walking to keep warm. It was difficult to make sense of these crimes and how they were tied to her abduction ten years ago.

In the distance, the rumbling sound of a train reverberated around her. Upon hearing a footstep behind her, she turned, expecting to see Cash. She opened her mouth to scream when she saw a man with a dark coat and ski mask standing behind her.

Before she could move or call out, something sharp pierced her chest. Looking down at the V opening in her coat, she was horrified to see two tiny barbs embedded in her sweater. Instantly her entire body spasmed with the force of an electric jolt.

Helpless, she fell to the ground, unable to move or shout for help. The dark eyes peering down at her from the openings in the mask appeared full of wicked satisfaction.

The stranger picked her up and turned, carrying her to the truck. The same black truck with tinted windows she and Cash had noticed earlier. She'd been so lost in thoughts of who might be behind this that she hadn't heard the vehicle behind her. The train may have masked the sound, too.

The killer dumped her in the back seat, then quickly got in behind the wheel. Seconds later, they were driving away.

No! This couldn't be happening! Jacy was shocked to realize this guy had been brazen enough to stake out his own crime scene just to get to her.

And she'd unwittingly walked right into his trap. With all the officers down at the creek bed, standing beneath the bridge, the road had been left wide open for anyone to drive by.

She wanted to cry and scream in frustration. Had

Cash seen her go down? Maybe overheard the sound of the Taser shooting barbs into her?

Or was she on her own?

Panic threatened to overwhelm her. Then she abruptly realized she wasn't alone. Cash had reminded her that God was always with her. A strange sense of calmness washed over her.

God was with her. And maybe this was all part of God's plan. Hadn't she asked Cash to set her up in a motel as bait?

Using her to draw the killer out of hiding hadn't been done intentionally, but she was right about the fact that doing so had worked.

Her being in the back seat of the truck was proof of that.

Okay, then. She swallowed hard against the ball of fear lodged in her throat. Her muscles were starting to loosen up and she opened and closed her fingers, still feeling weak. Overpowering the masked man probably wasn't an option.

No, what she needed to do was to keep this guy occupied until Cash and the other police officers involved in the case could find them.

It didn't matter if she died at this man's hands, as long as Cash and Detective Vargas found and arrested him.

The last thing she wanted was for this killer to continue going after young girls.

This nightmare had to end with her. No matter what.

"Where's Jacy?" Cash abruptly turned, scanning the ridge above. The creek bed was low enough that he couldn't see the entire road. The sound of a train grew louder as it approached. A wave of fear washed over him as he scrambled up the embankment.

The brief flash of taillights in the distance ramped up his terror. They were high enough to belong to a truck. Maybe even the same truck with the tinted windows they'd seen earlier that day.

"Jacy!" He whirled toward his SUV, intending to follow, when he saw a tiny metal barb lying on the ground.

Every cop had a Taser, something they used only in dire circumstances. He was sure this barb hadn't been here earlier; he'd have noticed it.

As would the other officers.

"Vargas! Jacy's been kidnapped! She was tased—get someone to grab the barb as evidence!" He shouted at the top of his lungs to be heard over the train. Without waiting for a response, he ran to the SUV. Only once he had the engine running and had hit the road did he reach for his phone to call his boss.

"What's up, Rawson?"

"I need a police chopper in the air, ASAP. We're looking for a black Ford truck with tinted windows heading west on Highway 21. Hurry, the killer has Jacy Urban."

"License plate?" Timmons asked.

"Negative. A temporary plate in the back window. I was too far away to get a number. Black Ford truck, with a crew cab, meaning it has a back seat. Tinted windows," he repeated.

"Understood. I'll get a police chopper in the air and alert the state patrol."

"Hurry!" Cash hit the gas hard, speeding as fast as possible while mentally kicking himself for allowing Jacy out of his sight. At the time, he'd thought it best that Jacy didn't listen as they'd discussed bringing cadaver dogs in to search the area under the bridge and along the frozen creek for Claire Simmons.

But now, the killer had her! And if he didn't find them soon, Jacy would end up just like Suzanna Perry. *Dead.*

No, please, Lord Jesus, don't take Jacy! The prayer reverberated through his mind as he desperately searched for the black truck.

His phone rang and he quickly grabbed it. "Rawson."

"This is FBI agent Kyle Boyd. I understand Jacy Urban is missing."

"Yes." Oddly, working through the case helped keep Cash's panic at bay. "We found Suzanna Perry's body beneath a bridge outside the small unincorporated town of Bakersville. She had been buried under a pile of rocks."

"I heard. What can I do to help?" Boyd asked.

"I need resources to find the black Ford truck with tinted windows." He glanced at the overcast sky, wishing the chopper was there already. "And it wouldn't hurt to set up a couple dozen roadblocks."

"I can assist with that. But what about information on our unsub? Did you or Jacy come up with anything on this guy?"

"Only the possibility that he's someone from her high school. Either a substitute teacher or a classmate. We started going through her yearbook, but didn't get to finish." An abrupt thought hit him. "Wait a minute, what about cross-referencing male students that shared a chemistry class with Jacy and who were also in the choir?"

"Why chemistry?" Boyd asked.

"The pepper spray and smoke bomb." It wasn't much of a connection, but it was all he could come up with. "Start there. If you don't find a connection, we'll have to broaden our search. But it seems like this guy knows how to use chemicals to his advantage, like the tranquilizer dart. I never heard back on the fingerprints or what drug was used but he fired tranq darts at us, twice. Plus, Jacy was taken on her way home from choir practice. I spoke to George Voight, the neighbor living in the house along her route. He mentioned that Jacy had stopped in front of his house and turned to look behind her. As if someone had called her name. It would make sense that the person was someone she knew."

There was a moment of silence as the FBI agent pondered the additional information. "Okay, I'll see what we can come up with. I'll follow up on the tranq dart, too. That's some good detective work there, Rawson. Stay in touch."

"Yeah, you, too." Cash dropped the phone in the cup holder, knowing he would not hesitate to use every possible resource at his disposal. He wanted hundreds of cops to swarm the highways, searching for the black truck.

Where was that chopper? They were roughly thirty minutes out of Madison, and it should be up in the sky by now.

What if they missed this guy? No, he couldn't let his thoughts go down that path. He couldn't bear the idea of losing Jacy.

He swallowed hard, sweeping the road for the truck. He'd known getting emotionally involved with Jacy wasn't smart. But he hadn't realized how far gone he was.

How much he truly cared.

His phone rang again and he snatched it from the cup holder. "Rawson."

"Where are you? Which direction did you want me to take?" Vargas's voice was all business.

"The truck headed west. That's the way I took, too. But for all I know, he's turned around by now." It made Cash feel sick to know he was stumbling around in the dark. "I'm waiting for a police chopper to head this way. That should help."

As if on cue, the faint *whomp, whomp* of a helicopter reached his ears. The bird was small in the distance, but as he watched, it grew larger. "It's in the air now. Black Ford truck with a crew cab, tinted windows and no plates."

"Got it, I'll head the other way. I've left a deputy in charge of the crime scene so we can free up everyone else to search."

"Thank you." He knew Vargas was taking a risk in leaving before the coroner got there, but a live victim always took priority over a dead one.

And he was determined to make sure Jacy survived this ordeal. She had to!

"Keep me updated," Vargas said before disconnecting from the call.

Cash wished they had something to go on. He told himself the police chopper would have the best chance of spotting the truck, but that was primarily if the killer stayed on the highways.

Even a chopper couldn't follow every backcountry road stretching across the state.

Or even across state lines.

The knot in his gut tightened at the thought of Jacy ending up in Minnesota, which would mean notifying their state police and possibly slowing things down as more officers became involved. As much as he liked the idea of extra searchers, he didn't want anything delaying him. Minnesota was the closest border, with Lake Michigan to the east. Illinois several hundred miles south.

Glancing at the dashboard clock, he assured himself there hadn't been time for this guy to get Jacy out of the state. Small comfort at this point.

Every truck he saw made his heart leap in his chest, only to crash when he realized it wasn't the black Ford.

Where were they? Where had the killer taken Jacy?

Ten years ago, Jacy had escaped, running across the highway only to end up at the bottom of a ravine. It occurred to him now that the killer may have a hiding spot somewhere nearby. Much like he must have had ten years ago.

And if that was the case? A chopper might not find the vehicle in time. If the black truck was well hidden, they wouldn't find this guy before he killed Jacy.

Cash grabbed his phone, desperate for an update. Thankfully, his lieutenant answered right away. "The chopper is in the air."

"I see it. But have you heard anything? They should have the truck in their sights by now."

"Not yet." Cash heard the murmur of voices from somewhere behind his boss. It made him think of the killer having access to a police radio. If that was the case, the driver of the black truck would have known about the chopper long before it arrived in the area.

"He may have gone into hiding somewhere close by." Cash tried not to sound as panicked as he felt. "I need officers to canvass the area within a fifty-mile radius."

"Fifty miles? That will take some time," Timmons warned. "I've freed up as many officers as possible and have alerted the state patrol."

"Please, get them spread out through the area." Cash wasn't above begging. "Our working theory is this guy has access to a police radio. If he knew about the chopper heading out to search for the truck, he'd find a place to take cover." There were so many acres of woods, small towns, and other possibilities for this guy to hide in. And the fact that this perp had left Suzanna's body here meant he was familiar with the area.

By far, more familiar with this neck of the woods than he was.

"Listen, Lieutenant, the truck is large, with a crew cab. Maybe too big to fit in some garages. But we might be able to find the vehicle if this perp simply parked off along the side of the road somewhere. We need to try."

"Understood. I'll see what we can do," Timmons promised.

The exchange with his boss had not been reassuring. Quite the opposite. They had no name to use as a reference point. Just a description of a vehicle that could already be well hidden off the road.

Gripping the steering wheel tightly, Cash estimated he'd gone about fifteen miles. He was uncharacteristically frozen by indecision. Should he keep going? Or leave the rest of the highway to the chopper? Maybe it was time to turn around and head down some of the side roads.

What should he do? *Please, Lord Jesus, guide me! Give me the strength and knowledge I need to find Jacy!*

An intersection up ahead helped make up his mind. He'd turn off there to see if he could find any clues.

If not, he'd retrace his path heading back toward the crime scene.

Driving around and hoping for the best didn't seem to be much of a plan. But he couldn't come up with another viable option. Not without more information to go on.

Cash slowed at the intersection, glancing in both directions. Which way should he go? North or south?

He decided to head north. There were miles of woods in that direction and fewer people living in the area, too. During the warm summer months there were plenty of city dwellers that would drive up from Madison, Milwaukee and Chicago to enjoy the rustic life in cabins or trailers near lakes and rivers. But in January? Not so much.

It would make sense that their unsub would take his victims somewhere isolated.

Where no one could hear their screams.

He slowed his pace so that he could look more closely for signs of a truck in the area. If the killer had been in a hurry, he may not have taken the time to mask his tracks the way Cash had when they'd hidden in the trees to escape the truck.

But he didn't find anything.

Don't give up hope. The silent lecture reverberated through his mind. *Don't give up hope!*

When his phone rang, he pounced on it. "Rawson."

"Agent Boyd. Does the name Robert White mean anything to you?"

Cash's pulse spiked. "No, should it? Is he our possible unsub?"

"Maybe, but it's thin. The guy was in Jacy's chemistry class and in the choir. He's a year older than her, making him a junior at the time she was a sophomore. I'm not sure they had many other classes together." Boyd paused before adding, "I can't lie, I'm having trouble imagining a seventeen-year-old perp grabbing young women and killing them."

"You're a fed, you know some serial killers begin early, killing their pets before moving on to people." Cash hated the thought of this Robert White having Jacy. "Maybe this guy was on an expedited track."

"It's possible. I'm searching the databases now to see if this guy has any property in the area."

"Hurry," Cash urged. "The chopper hasn't found the black truck yet, and I'm worried he's already fallen off-grid."

"Will do." Boyd ended the call.

Having a possible name to work with was great, but only if they had identified the right guy and there was some way the name would lead them to Jacy.

Before it was too late!

THIRTEEN

When the truck bounced over deep ruts nearly sending her rolling off the back seat and onto the floor, Jacy realized they'd left the road. Her spirits sank, knowing that this would make it so much harder for Cash to find her.

As if that wouldn't be a nearly impossible task, anyway.

There wasn't a doubt in her mind Cash would try to locate them; he was dedicated and determined. Yet her abductor seemed to have a plan. She wondered if he'd left Suzanna's body in such an obvious place solely to draw her and Cash to the area.

The jostling continued for several long minutes. Being tased had left her weak and shaky. She'd considered trying to overpower the killer while he was driving, but then had thought it better to wait.

At some point, they'd reach their destination. Jacy took several deep calming breaths, silently praying for strength. Once her abductor stopped the truck, she'd use the opportunity to escape.

She hoped.

Doing her best to act like a rag doll, she allowed

herself to be bounced around as if she couldn't control herself. Whoever this guy was, she wanted—no, *needed* him to believe she was no threat.

She didn't have any weapons of any kind. The only thing working in her favor was the element of surprise. If that didn't work? She swallowed hard against the lump in the back of her throat.

If she didn't escape him, she knew he'd strangle her to death.

Just like he'd killed Suzanna Perry, and probably the other missing girls, too.

She prayed as they continued bouncing over the uneven turf. Her biggest fear was that this guy would succeed in killing her while avoiding being caught.

Leaving him free to kill again.

After what seemed like eons, her abductor stopped the truck. She continued to lie limp along the back seat, although it wasn't easy to hide her tension as she waited for him to open the door to drag her out.

"We're home," he said in a singsong tone.

There was something familiar about his voice, but she told herself it didn't matter. The moment he pushed open his door, she bolted upright and grabbed the door handle on the opposite side from where he was. She half fell out of the truck, her muscles weaker than she'd realized.

"Jacy! Get back here!"

His tone wasn't singsong now. He was mad. But so was she. She saw the large shed and knew that he would soon hide the truck inside, out of sight from anyone passing by.

She ran away from the shed, as fast as her legs could carry her. That, unfortunately, wasn't saying much. For a moment, she thought she was running through darkness, but no, it was still daylight.

Then she realized that this attempt to escape was exactly the same way she'd run from her captor ten years ago.

She was surprised at how the brief memory had flashed in her mind. Still, she concentrated on running across the deeply rutted field toward a patch of trees not far away.

Hurry, hurry! Jacy used a zigzag pattern while she ran, mentally bracing herself for the sound of gunfire. Somehow, she knew the masked man would not give up as easily as he had ten years ago.

She heard a pop then something sharp hit her between the shoulder blades. She stumbled and pushed on, ignoring the pain. But her muscles went lax and the next thing she knew, she was facedown on the ground.

He'd hit her with the tranq gun! She wanted to cry as she struggled to drag herself forward.

"Did you really think you could get away from me so easily?" Her captor made a tsk-tsk sound. She lifted her head, trying to look at him, but her vision blurred.

Then darkness enveloped her.

Jacy had no idea how long she had been knocked out. But when she opened her eyes, she realized she was in an old stuffy house. The sofa she was lying upon smelled musty and stale.

Yet she was surprisingly warm. The scent of burning wood wafted toward her.

It took a few minutes for her to remember everything that had transpired. Suzanna Perry's dead body with the dark bruises around her neck, being tased and then trying to escape only to be brought down by a dart fired from a tranquilizer gun.

A wave of despair hit hard.

How long had she been there? She carefully glanced around without moving too much, searching for her abductor. Too long, she thought grimly.

Cash hadn't found her, and that was discouraging, too. Yet she tried not to dwell on that.

Strange that her captor had bothered to keep her alive, especially after the way he'd fired recklessly at them at Cash's house. As she'd run across the field, she'd fully expected to be shot down by a bullet.

Not drugged.

The inconsistencies in his actions didn't make sense. Then again, nothing about this guy was logical. Maybe his temper had gotten the better of him back at Cash's place.

Now, the killer had her right where he wanted her.

Her mouth was cotton-dry, no doubt from whatever drug he'd put in the dart. She felt certain that her coat had helped dilute the amount she'd absorbed into her bloodstream. From the dim light coming in through dirty windows, she had to assume she'd only lost an hour, maybe two at the most.

Unless it was already the next day?

"Ah, I see you're starting to wake up." The oddly familiar voice came from behind her. Jacy slowly turned from her supine position on the sofa to look back over her shoulder.

Then gasped as the killer's face came into view.

"Robbie?" His name came out in a hoarse whisper. Instantly a cascade of memories washed over her. Robbie White had been a good friend of hers throughout her freshman and into her sophomore years of high school. They'd never dated and, as far as she'd known, he'd never been interested in her in that way.

But looking at him now, she remembered the night ten years ago when he'd called out to her on the street. He'd asked for her help because his van was stuck in a ditch along the side of the highway. They'd walked over a mile to get there. She'd just gotten suspicious and had slowed down when he'd suddenly grabbed her wrists behind her back and tried to force her into the vehicle. He'd harshly whispered into her ear, *I've waited long enough, Jacy!*

Horrified by his intent, she'd wrenched out of his grip and run. His fingers had closed over her coat sleeves, but she'd managed to shed the garment, pulling her arms free from the jacket and sprinting away from him as fast as she could.

Incomprehensible to realize her close friend had done this. Not just trying to abduct her ten years ago, but everything that had happened since.

No wonder she hadn't wanted to remember. The pain of Robbie's betrayal had been too much.

"Well, well, I always wondered why you never sketched me." Robbie's face held an ugly, leering grin. She'd easily recognized him, even though he looked much different now than he had when they were younger.

Ten years ago, Robbie had carried extra pounds on his frame, worn thick glasses and had suffered from eczema. The man standing before her had lost a good fifty pounds and wore contacts instead of glasses. Although, looking closer, she could tell he still had a red rash along the side of his neck.

"According to the newspapers, you didn't know who'd taken you that night," he continued. "But I always wondered if deep down you had known. Especially after I learned you'd gone to work as a police sketch artist." He let out a creepy laugh. "Did you like how I blinded you with the pepper spray and smoke bomb? Genius, huh?"

Lunatic was a better word, but she didn't say it. "I didn't know it was you—my memory was blocked until today. And I still don't understand why you would want to hurt me!" She weakly pushed herself up on her elbows. "We were friends, Robbie. Friends!"

"You knew I wanted more." He took another step toward her, his fingers opening and then closing into fists. She wondered if he'd punch her before he'd assault and strangle her. "But I wasn't good enough for you then. I was too heavy, not cool enough." He sneered. "You and all the other pretty girls acted as if I didn't exist. But I do, Jacy. Every single girl I ever talked to didn't see me. Didn't seem to notice me as a man. Not even Beth, my next-door neighbor who went to Drake." His lips curled. "I had no choice but to take them by force."

She grappled with how to respond. It was true she hadn't been interested in Robbie as a boyfriend, but they had still been friends.

Or so she'd thought. But, clearly, she'd been wrong. So very wrong.

"I valued our friendship, Robbie." She met his stare head-on, hoping to reach the boy she once knew. "You were important to me. But this?" She waved a hand at their rustic surroundings. She had no idea where they were, but it was someplace that he'd found abandoned or a house he'd purchased. He had lived in the rich sub-division, after all, with the car his parents had bought for him. "Friends don't hurt each other like this. They don't try to kill each other."

"What do you know about it?" The disdain was evident in his tone. "I wanted more from you, Jacy. You dated that lame Steve idiot, who didn't deserve you. Did you turn to me then? No, you didn't. Because you were too blind to see what was right in front of you." His face reddened with anger, making the eczema stand out in blotches. "Well, guess what? I'm in charge now. And you won't be blind anymore. I intend to take what is rightfully mine." He flashed an eerie smile. "You, Jacy. I want you."

What? No! She tried not to recoil in disgust at the very thought of him touching her. Struggling to remain calm, she thought there had to be a way to get through to him.

"Robbie, do you remember when I dropped my food tray in the cafeteria the first week of school?" She held his gaze, hoping and praying that reminding him of their former friendship would prevent him from hurting her.

A lame plan, considering he'd killed so many other girls, each one looking just like her. It was depressing to realize he'd specifically chosen these other girls to assault and kill because of her.

Because she was the one who'd gotten away.

When he didn't answer, she continued, "You were so sweet, Robbie. You helped me clean up the mess, then bought me a replacement lunch, because I didn't have enough money. I was so happy to have your help, especially from someone a grade ahead of me. That was the first day we became friends, do you remember?"

She'd expected to see a flash of compassion in his eyes but found them to be cold and hard and bitter. In that moment, she knew the classmate she'd once considered a friend was gone forever.

Leaving a cold-blooded serial killer in his place.

Every muscle in Cash's body was tight as he continued searching for the black truck.

Too much time had passed for this guy to still be out on the highways. No, Cash firmly believed he was holed up somewhere with Jacy.

He reached for his phone, intending to call Agent Boyd again, when it rang. He quickly answered, "Rawson."

"We know more about this perp," Boyd said. "Robert White did a little over seven years in jail for an attempted sexual assault in Illinois. He was caught thanks to the work of a forensic sketch artist who worked with the victim."

Cash whistled under his breath. "Jacy Urban is a forensic artist."

"I know. Interesting, isn't it? When White was released, he reported to his parole officer for six months as ordered before he disappeared. There's an outstanding warrant for his arrest in Illinois for violating the rules of his parole." There was a brief pause before Boyd noted, "Oh, and he's listed on the sex offender registry. Apparently the DA insisted on this as part of his parole because the girl he'd assaulted had been sixteen at the time."

Again, just like Jacy. And the other missing girls.

White had a pattern, that's for sure. While the additional information was interesting, and explained the gap in White's crime spree, it didn't help them now. They needed to find his current location. "You mentioned searching the property in the area for any links to White."

"I have, came up empty." Boyd let out a sigh of frustration. "I've tried his mother's maiden name, too, but that didn't give us anything, either. His parents died, leaving him a nice sum of money, though. It's possible he was able to buy something under a different name."

The keen sense of despair was staggering. Cash tried not to let it crush him. He would not give up hope that they'd locate her. "There must be a way to find him, Boyd. He and that truck of his didn't disappear into thin air."

"My next task is to search every property in the area where the owner hasn't paid any property taxes. Maybe he is using one of them."

It was a good idea. Those who abandon their places, either because of death without heirs or just moving on, didn't continue to pay their taxes. And if there wasn't anyone to go after, the property just sat in limbo. Especially if there wasn't a lien from a bank or other financial institution. "Okay, keep it within this fifty-mile radius for now. I want those addresses, ASAP. I'll get other officers to help search every property you send over."

"Will do," Boyd agreed.

"Thanks." Cash set the phone aside, his eyes raking the area. He stared at the GPS screen for a moment, refamiliarizing himself with his location.

He'd taken so many back roads that he was worried he'd gone too far off track.

Every minute that passed by without news from anyone in law enforcement was agony. Their search was taking too long. He winced when he realized two hours had passed since Jacy had gone missing from the rocky creek bed beneath the bridge where they'd found Suzanna Perry's body.

Two hours!

He took a moment to look closer at the map of the area. He didn't want to go over the same ground he already had, but still felt that it was more likely White had stayed north and west of where they were, only because the area was more rural, making it easier to hide.

But what if Cash was wrong? What if Robert White was smarter than they were giving him credit for being? After all, he'd avoided being caught for this long.

But not in Illinois, he reminded himself. No, he'd been caught before and had served jail time. He should have been connected to the girls missing in Wisconsin, but hadn't been. A lapse he would take up the chain of command.

After they found him.

Cash blinked, bringing the map back into focus. Enough second-guessing himself. He'd always depended on his gut instincts to lead him.

And, of course, he'd always put his trust and faith in God.

Feeling better, he decided to go another ten miles west before turning and heading farther north. That would take him along the outer limits of his self-imposed fifty-mile search radius.

Glad to have a firm destination in mind, Cash headed

for the next intersection. Turning right, he took a narrow winding road.

His phone rang and he quickly grabbed it. "Boyd? Do you have an address?"

"This is Vargas. I just heard that the cadaver dog has found Claire Simmons's body. She has the same dark bruises around her throat. Both bodies are being taken to the ME's office in Appleton."

It was tempting to ask for them to be transferred to Madison, just because the city was bigger and their ME probably had more experience, but he held his tongue. His main concern was Jacy. "Thanks for letting me know."

"Believe it or not, that jerk buried her on the other side of the bridge," Vargas said in disgust. "Officers were already scouring that area when the dog arrived. Took him less than two minutes to alert on Claire."

At this point, Cash would believe just about anything. "You know, I was thinking about the way he chose that location. Almost as if he fully intended for us to uncover those bodies."

"Even though the town of Bakersville is unincorporated?" Vargas asked, his tone tinged with doubt. "I don't know about that. If not for the dog finding Suzanna, we'd still be stumbling around in the dark."

"Yeah, but he also took Jacy from there. I'm convinced he has a police scanner that he's using to get information. And what's even more interesting is that he was able to get to the bridge so quickly." Cash perused both sides of the road. "All of that reinforces my thought that he has Jacy stashed somewhere close by."

"You mentioned getting an address?" Vargas asked.

"The feds are running a search on abandoned properties in the area. Those where the owners haven't paid their property taxes in the past few years." He glanced at the clock, silently acknowledging that only ten minutes had passed since he'd spoken to Boyd. "I'll need resources to search the abandoned properties once we have specific locations to work with."

"Understood, I'll help in any way I can," Vargas said. Cash knew the Appleton detective would want justice for the two dead girls they'd found. "Where are you now?"

"I'm on highway RR, which appears to be in the middle of nowhere Wisconsin."

"Unfortunately, there are a lot of wide-open spaces like that." Vargas exhaled then instructed, "Keep me updated."

"You, too." Cash was somewhat relieved that Claire had been found. At least both girls' parents would be able to give their daughters a proper burial.

He hoped and prayed that the other girls' bodies would be found soon, too.

What if Robert White wasn't the right guy? If they'd gone down the wrong path, they may be missing a piece of property that was currently being used and paid for by the real killer.

The wave of doubt was difficult to ignore.

Tire tracks caught his eye. Cash hit the brake, bringing the SUV to a jarring stop. Was he imagining them? The hard-packed earth made it difficult to see the path clearly. He closed his eyes for a moment then opened them again.

Yeah, those were tire tracks all right. Barely there, he had to admit, but visible enough to raise his suspicions.

Especially since the tire tracks appeared to end at a large shed where he imagined the truck may have been hidden inside. Looking behind the structure, he noticed a farmhouse.

And smoke curling from the chimney.

Without hesitation, he continued driving along the road until he found a grove of trees. There, he parked and grabbed his phone. He tried Boyd first, but the fed didn't answer. He left a message with a rough location and then called Vargas.

"I'm forty minutes out," Vargas said. "Wait for me."

"Get here as soon as you can." Cash ended the call without promising to wait.

Forty minutes? That was time he didn't have. He put the phone on silent, left the keys on the driver's seat, then made his way through the trees.

No way would he let anything stop him from getting to Jacy as soon as possible.

FOURTEEN

Keep him talking.

The mantra had echoed through her mind since she'd regained consciousness. Jacy knew that stalling for time was the only thing she could do to get out of this mess.

She detested everything about Robbie and hearing him gloat about his crimes turned her stomach, but she did her best to string him along, anyway.

Secretly praying he wouldn't be able to kill her, the way he had the others. If she made herself human in his eyes, reminding him of the friendship they'd shared, maybe, just maybe, he wouldn't be able to do it.

A vain hope, but it was all she could come up with.

"Robbie, if I had known you wanted to go out on a date, I would have gladly accepted your offer." She put on a concerned smile. The statement was a bald-faced lie, but she held his gaze anyway, hoping he'd believe her. She looked briefly at the black gun he had tucked in the waistband of his jeans, but she didn't allow her eyes to linger. The last thing she wanted was to give him an excuse to use it. "We were always friends, Robbie. I had no idea you wanted something more."

"That's because you didn't *see* me." He scowled, curling his lip as he paced the length of the living room with jerky movements. He was clearly unstable, which only made the entire situation more terrifying. Jacy sensed it wouldn't take much for him to go over the edge. "All the pretty girls were blind when it came to me. Because I was a rash-covered fat kid with thick glasses. I was invisible to every single one of you!"

"High school is difficult," Jacy admitted. "And you are right about how some kids were cruel. But I wasn't mean to you, Robbie. Not once. And now, as an adult, you know that those measly four years of high school don't matter."

"Maybe not to you," he sneered.

"You're a good-looking guy, Robbie. You've changed for the better." Another lie, as he was evil personified, but she did her best to sound admiring. "Is that how you got those other girls—Suzanna and Claire—to go with you? Did you charm them into going along to your truck?"

A ghastly smile creased his features. "Yeah. They didn't look down their noses at me, the way you did, Jacy. And, really, once I had them in my clutches, I didn't mind listening to their screams. When I put my fingers around their throat, they looked into my eyes. That's when they finally saw me."

Screams? She shivered, despite her efforts not to show her abhorrence. She tried not to dwell on the pain both girls had suffered at Robbie's hands. "I never looked down my nose at you," she protested, because that much was true. "We were friends, Robbie. I valued our time together. You were one of the few people I could always talk to."

"Yeah, you talked to me about the guys you were interested in. Any guy but me, right?" He stopped his pacing and stepped closer to the sofa. Then he reached out to touch a strand of her hair. "You cut your hair. I don't like it."

"I can grow it long again if you'd like," she forced herself to say. It took every ounce of willpower not to shrink from his touch.

"The fact that you don't even remember when I tried to hold your hand proves you never saw me. That you never, ever, would have agreed to go out with me." He abruptly yanked hard on her hair, the sharp pain bringing tears to her eyes. "For a police sketch artist, you don't see people clearly at all, do you?"

There was a kernel of truth to his words. She hadn't seen this part of him, that much was for certain. "How did you know I was a sketch artist?" Blinking away her tears, she silently willed him to back off. "And how did you find that sketch I did? The one you slid under my apartment door with the eyes gouged out?"

"I used the jail computer to find out all about you, Jacy." He mercifully dropped her hair and took a step back. "I found out you were a police sketch artist and that you lived in Appleton. That was the main reason I got myself a couple of police scanners. To help track your movements." The fact that he'd found her personal information so easily was concerning, but she pushed that thought away to focus on Robbie.

"After I was released on parole, I made a plan to come and find you." His smile only made him look evil. "Once I was able to secure a fake ID, the rest was easy. I stole a truck and found a place to stay. I couldn't believe it when I came across your sketch at the technical school campus. Signing JC in the corner, rather than the initials of your first and last name was clever. But I still knew the artist was you."

Horrifying to realize how far he'd gone to track her down. And she felt certain that the reason he'd gouged out the eyes on the sketch was that she didn't "see" him clearly.

Keep him talking! "That was really smart of you to do all of that. But I'm curious, Robbie. Did you set the fire to our old high school? And what made you target Suzanna and Claire?"

"I set the fire, although I realize now that was a dumb risk. I thought maybe I could distract the police attention from my plans, but that didn't work." His eyes narrowed. "As far as the girls? I had been in jail a long time, eight years, since it took nine months for me to be sentenced. I deserved Claire and Suzanna. I deserved to feel alive again."

So he could only feel alive when he was killing young innocent girls? Because that's when they truly saw him? His twisted logic made her stomach churn with nausea. Or maybe it was the drug she'd absorbed. Likely both.

Either way, Jacy tried hard not to gag.

He abruptly swung toward her, the move causing her to rear back against the sofa instinctively. "Enough talking. I've been waiting a long time for this."

No! Please, no! She swallowed the scream that threatened to overwhelm her. A glimpse of movement through the window behind him gave her pause.

Someone was out there! Cash?

Her pulse spiked with anticipation.

"Wait. Could I please have some water?" She slid higher up along the sofa, so that she was in more of a sitting position rather than stretched out on her back. She still felt weak and shaky, thanks to the drug and tasing, but she intended to be ready if Cash was able to get her out of there. "Please, there's no reason to fight with me, Robbie. You don't need to hurt me. I care about you. I'm glad I'm here with you."

A flicker of distrust darkened his stare. His obsession with her was completely irrational, but she didn't think it would hurt to play along.

At least for now.

"Please, Robbie?" She smiled, tucking the strand of hair he'd cruelly yanked behind her ear. "Just a sip of water would be great."

For a long moment, she thought he'd refuse, but he turned and crossed to the kitchen sink. After filling a dirty glass halfway, he brought it over. "Here."

She readily accepted the glass. Particles of dust from the rarely used glass floated in the water, but she took a sip anyway, briefly closing her eyes while praying she wouldn't choke on it. To her surprise, the water was soothing against her dry mouth and throat, despite the dust tainting it.

"Thank you," she murmured. She wanted to look out the window again but didn't because of the intensity of Robbie's glare.

How much longer could she hold him off from attacking her?

She swung her legs over so that she was sitting upright on the sofa, her feet on the floor. She took another cautious sip of the water while surreptitiously sweeping her eyes over the room, searching for something to use as a weapon. There was nothing obvious in sigh.

Maybe a log for the fire, but the stove was located behind the sofa. She didn't dare turn to look that way. Tightening her grip on the glass, she struggled to act normal.

Every muscle in her body was tense, although she tried not to show it. She fully intended to be ready to make her move the moment Cash did.

But the waiting was agony. Had she imagined the flash of movement? What if she had, and Cash wasn't really out there at all?

She drew in a deep breath, trying not to panic.

Please, Lord, give me strength!

"Enough." Robbie reached out as if to grab the glass from her fingers.

She instinctively tossed the rest of the water in his face then threw the glass directly at the bridge of his nose. He reared backward, raising his hands and yelling in pain as the glass struck his face.

That momentary distraction was all she needed. Bolting off the sofa, she sprinted toward the door, desperate to escape. She yanked the door open and ran outside into the fresh air. Hearing the thumping footsteps behind her provided the surge of adrenaline she desperately needed.

She ran, barreling out over the snow-spotted rocky terrain as fast as she could. Her strength was not nearly up to par, though. Not the way it was when she'd run from Robbie ten years ago.

Hurry! She had to get away!

"Jacy!" Cash's shout made her want to weep in relief.

"Look out!" she shouted, running toward the shed. "Robbie has a gun!"

As if on cue, the sound of a gunshot reverberated around her.

She intuitively slowed her pace, fearing Cash had been targeted. What if Robbie had hit him?

No! Cash!

"Go, Jacy! Go!" Cash shouted as a second gunshot echoed through the air.

With a sob, she forced herself to keep running, stumbling over rocks, rutted dirt and fallen branches, yet managing to stay upright. Deep down, she understood she was Robbie's ultimate prize.

And once she was out of the way, Cash would have a much better chance of taking Robbie down.

There was an eerie silence behind her as she reached the relative safety of the trees. She risked a quick glance over her shoulder but didn't see anyone.

Where were Robbie and Cash? She didn't know.

Jacy slowed her pace as tree branches snagged at her clothing and her hair. Her breath sawed in and out of her lungs as she fought the urge to collapse on the ground. The drug Robbie had used in the dart was still not completely out of her system.

She continued pushing forward.

Hoping and praying there would be more officers swarming the farmhouse at any moment.

Ignoring the pain in his thigh from where White's bullet had grazed him, Cash took cover along the side of the shed. He was glad to see that Jacy had kept running toward the trees. Her safety had been his priority.

But now that she was out of harm's way? He would not rest until he had Robert White in custody. Hearing her refer to him as Robbie had been jarring. She'd obviously known White, and fairly well to use his nickname.

There wasn't time to worry about their relationship now.

He wasn't sure how long it would take Vargas and the others to arrive. Once he'd validated the black truck was in the shed, he'd rendered the vehicle useless by slashing all four tires, grimly noting the police scanner mounted to the dashboard. Once that task was accomplished, he'd crept closer for a better look at the house.

The only way White was getting away from the farmhouse was on foot. Or on a stretcher. Either way worked for him, as long as the guy was in handcuffs.

"I'm Detective Cash Rawson," he shouted. "Throw down your weapon."

No response.

He tried again. "Robert White, you're under arrest for kidnapping and murder. Throw down your weapon!"

Still nothing. He stifled a sigh. It wasn't really a surprise that White would force this to go down the hard way.

He eased up to the edge of the shed and quickly peered around the corner. There was no sign of White, which concerned him.

Weapon in hand, he rounded the shed and half limped and half ran toward the house. Pressing his back against the wall of the old structure, he listened intently.

Hearing nothing but silence.

A flash of panic hit hard. Where was he? Hiding inside? Waiting for Cash to show himself?

Praying Vargas would get there soon, Cash made his way around to the back of the farmhouse. He gingerly tested several windows as he went, but they all seemed to be painted or possibly nailed shut.

Going in through the front door was not an option— the space looked too open, making him an easy target. He wanted to apprehend White, not be shot in the chest by him.

He stumbled across a rear door, one that faced a half caved-in barn. Testing the handle, he was relieved that it turned.

Someone had come this way recently. White? Escaping from the house? Maybe.

He eased the door open and stepped inside. Sweeping his gaze over the floor, he didn't see any damp footprints, indicating someone had come this way.

Keeping his weapon ready, he continued sneaking through the house. There were bedrooms along both sides of the narrow hallway, forcing him to stop and peer into each one to make sure White wasn't waiting there. To his surprise, he found another police scanner in one of the bedrooms.

Up ahead, he could see the living room and kitchen. But no sign of White. Could he have missed him? Was the guy outside hiding behind the dilapidated barn?

Cash stepped on a board that groaned beneath his weight. Horrified at the noise, he ducked just as more gunfire echoed through the house. At least two bullets shattered flimsy and half-rotten drywall, forcing him to crawl into one of the bedrooms.

"Shooting a cop isn't smart," Cash shouted, glad to know White was still inside. "You're only racking up more jail time. Guess you liked being in the slammer, huh?"

More bullets pelted the walls, sending bits of plaster and paint raining upon him.

Huddled in the far corner, he mentally counted the shots. He hadn't gotten a good look at White's weapon, but had surmised it to be a handgun. That meant the guy might be getting low on ammunition, if he wasn't almost out already.

There had been at least seven shots here, and at least four back at his house.

The most common handgun was a .38 and those only held five to six rounds. A 9-millimeter Luger could hold up to eighteen.

A Glock, the second most common handgun, held fifteen rounds.

Considering he'd counted ten to eleven shots so far, he was hoping White had a Glock without a spare clip.

"Come on, White," he goaded. "Give it up already. The house is going to be swarming with cops at any second." He prayed that was true. "Toss down your weapon and walk forward with your hands on your head to avoid getting hurt."

Two more bullets punctured the wall.

He'd only fired one round at White. While he wasn't happy he'd missed the guy, he was glad he still had a full clip. Eventually, White would run out of ammo.

It was only a matter of time.

The silence stretched, making him wonder if White was already out of bullets. Sliding across the floor toward the doorway, he risked a glance down the hall.

There was no sign of the killer.

Using the wall as support, he rose to his feet. Blood stained the floor, dripping down his leg from the thigh wound. Refusing to let the injury hold him back, he eased carefully down the hall.

Keeping his back flat against the wall, Cash peered toward the kitchen. The prolonged silence was unnerving, making him think White was attempting to draw him into a trap.

Honestly? It was working.

He took another step, listening acutely when the rumble of a car engine reached his ears.

Vargas?

The sound of a horn blasting made him frown. Vargas, or other officers, wouldn't sound off the horn.

But he imagined Jacy would.

He saw a flicker of movement from the other side of the sofa, giving him the impression that White was crouched behind the furniture, using the worn cushions as a shield.

"Throw down your weapon!" Cash shouted again.

The horn abruptly stopped and he prayed Jacy wasn't planning on coming inside. The barrel of White's gun eased up over the edge of the sofa, forcing Cash to duck down and hit the floor.

White didn't fire, though, and Cash wasn't sure if that was because he was out of ammo or simply preserving what he had left.

Seeing the gun was enough for him to react and

made him mad. Cash fired several rounds at the top of the sofa, knowing his bullets wouldn't likely reach their target. The best he could hope for was that returning gunfire would keep White pinned down in the living area long enough for Vargas to arrive.

The horn sounded again. Jacy's attempts to save him were exasperating, even though he was touched by her efforts.

He'd wanted her long gone from the area, not pulling up to the house in his SUV, sounding the horn.

The blaring sound stopped and he listened intently, apprehensively wondering what White would decide to do next.

Would he make a run for it out the front door, rushing toward Jacy?

Or jump up to fire his last few bullets at Cash?

The latter. As soon as the thought registered, he scooted backward, trying to get out of the way. The barrel of the gun came up first, followed by White.

"Got you," White said with a creepy grin. Then he pulled the trigger.

Cash had hugged the wall as much as possible but it wasn't enough to avoid being a target. The bullet from White's gun slammed into his shoulder, sending a tidal wave of pain washing over him and rendering his right arm useless.

The gun in his right hand fell to the floor, his arm numb.

White laughed again. Cash braced himself for another shot, but this time there was only a metallic click.

He was out of ammunition!

The pain was excruciating, but Cash shifted so that

he could grab the gun with his left hand. He lifted it and fired. Only, he was a fraction of a second too late.

White dove for the doorway. Cash's bullet went wide, hitting the door frame instead of his intended target. White disappeared outside.

No! Jacy!

Cash pushed himself to his feet and staggered toward the door, desperate to stop him.

FIFTEEN

Jacy had been relieved to find Cash's SUV, including the keys lying on the driver's seat. She knew Cash expected her to drive away, maybe to get help, but she couldn't leave him.

Not when she knew exactly what Robbie was capable of.

Hearing the gunfire from inside the farmhouse had been horrifying. She had no way of knowing if Cash had been hit.

Or if he was even still alive.

Driving up toward the house and leaning hard on the horn was the only distraction she could come up with.

What if it wasn't enough?

As that thought flickered through her head, more gunfire reverberated from the house. Then the front door opened and Robbie ran out, heading straight for her!

She hit the gas, causing the SUV to lurch forward. Robbie lifted his gun, pointing it at her. The windshield would not prevent a bullet, so she did the only thing she could think of.

Holding the steering wheel tightly, she aimed the

front of the SUV toward him. She'd never purposefully struck a pedestrian in her life, but that didn't stop her from attempting to strike Robbie.

The man who'd ruthlessly killed at least two young girls.

"Stop!" he shouted, his face twisting into a mask of anger. He managed to sidestep the vehicle, reaching out to grab the handle of her driver's door, trying to wrench it open.

Thankfully, it was locked.

"No!" Using all her strength, she cranked the steering wheel hard, making a tight circle. As she did so, Robbie thumped his fist on the window with such force, she feared he'd break it.

Another gunshot echoed. Robbie turned to look back at the house. Following his eyes, she saw Cash leaning heavily on the door frame, holding his gun, the barrel pointing at Robbie. She quickly noticed Cash was pale and bleeding.

He'd been hit!

Robbie started running away from the house. No! He couldn't escape! Hitting the gas again, she drove over the rutted ground directly toward Robbie. He was fast and she worried he'd make it to the trees before she could reach him.

Pressing the accelerator harder, the SUV lurched forward. The front bumper struck Robbie in the back of his thighs with enough force to knock him down. She winced as the SUV continued rolling over him.

She hit the brake mere inches from the grove of trees, feeling a little sick at knowing Robbie was pinned beneath the SUV.

Unable to bring herself to drive backward and roll

over him again, she opened the driver's-side door and jumped out. "Cash! Are you okay?"

A hand abruptly grabbed her ankle, yanking hard and pulling her off balance. Robbie was still alive!

Holding on to the door with both hands, she struggled to free herself from Robbie's grip. But he held on, pulling hard enough that her fingers began to slip from the door. "Cash!"

She saw Cash hit the ground. Had he passed out from blood loss? The pressure of Robbie pulling on her made her shin ache from hitting the lower edge of the SUV.

Then more gunfire sounded. Several shots in a row, without any hesitation between them.

The hands around her ankle let go. Swallowing a sob, she staggered away from the SUV, running to Cash, who was lying on his stomach, his left hand still holding the gun.

"Call 9-1-1," he told her breathlessly. "I think I hit him, but we need backup."

"Robbie took my phone." She knelt on the ground beside Cash. "You're hurt, Cash. We need an ambulance!"

"Pull out my phone, call 9-1-1." His voice sounded even more breathless now. "Hurry."

Patting his pockets, she found his phone. When she pulled it out, she heard a vehicle in the distance. She turned to stare at the squad car that was making its way across the field heading directly for them.

"Cash? Looks like the police are here."

"Vargas. Finally." Cash didn't turn his head to look; his gaze was trained on the narrow space beneath the

SUV up ahead. "Go meet with him, let him know White is here."

She was torn between wanting to stay by Cash to offer whatever first aid she could, and doing what he asked. The thought of getting more help swayed her toward running out to meet Vargas.

Standing in the field, waving her arms, she pointed at the SUV, hoping Vargas would understand what she was trying to say.

Then she scowled, noticing some movement within the trees. She blinked, hoping she'd imagined it. Was it possible Robbie hadn't been shot? That he'd only let her go to escape?

Acting on instinct and a deep desire to make sure Robbie paid for his crimes, Jacy turned and ran for the trees. "He's getting away!"

"No, Jacy, stay back!" Cash's voice was weak. There was no way he'd be able to chase Robbie down.

But she could.

Behind her, the sound of a siren blared. Vargas probably, but she ignored it.

As she grew closer to the trees, she saw Robbie limping away. Surprisingly, the gun was no longer in his grip, and one of his arms hung loose at his side. A spurt of anger hit hard and she increased her pace, gaining on him.

He glanced back at her then sneered as if he wasn't the least bit worried about her being there. She put on another burst of speed, then launched herself at him, tackling him as if she was a linebacker for the Green Bay Packers. She flattened him to the ground, doing her best to keep him pinned in place.

"Jacy!" Vargas shouted at her.

"Get off me," Robbie snarled, bucking to dislodge her.

Her body slid to the side, but she quickly tried to straighten herself on top of him. He wore a hoodie sweatshirt, so she grabbed the back of the hood and pulled with every ounce of strength she possessed, causing pressure around his neck.

He sputtered and gagged. Then he grasped the edge of the fabric with his good hand, using his fingertips to ease the pressure. Bucking again only caused her to move back farther, tightening the neckline of the sweatshirt even more around his neck.

"Jacy!" Vargas was there now, his weapon in hand. "Keep a hold of him until I can get him cuffed."

She gave a jerky nod, doing her best to do just that.

Vargas knelt beside them, grabbing Robbie's uninjured wrist and slapping a metal handcuff over it.

"Okay, slide over now," Vargas directed.

Jacy did as he asked, and he took control, putting all his weight on Robbie's back until he had both wrists cuffed behind him. She let go of the sweatshirt, and moved farther away, breathing hard from exertion.

"Robert White, you're under arrest for kidnapping and first-degree murder," Vargas said. "You have the right to remain silent. Anything you say can and will be used against you in a court of law." The detective continued reciting the Miranda warning as he hauled Robbie to his feet.

"I'm hurt," Robbie whined. "I was shot twice by that cop! In my arm and my leg."

"Yeah, I see that." Vargas tugged on him, drawing him in the direction of the police car sitting in the middle of the field. "But since you were strong enough to run into the trees, I think you'll make it to the squad car."

Robbie turned to stab her with a look of pure malice.

She scrambled to her feet, holding his gaze, letting him know she'd won their skirmish. She made sure he could see how glad she was to know he'd rot in jail for the rest of his life.

Then she thought about Cash and hurried back to where he'd been lying on the ground. To her horror, he was still there, only the gun was on the ground, having fallen from his grip.

"Cash!" She dropped to her knees to feel for a pulse. Cash didn't move, obviously unconscious. Her heart squeezed painfully in her chest. "Vargas! Cash is wounded! Call for an ambulance!"

"I did. It's on the way." Vargas opened the back door of his squad car, and shoved Robbie inside. Then he closed the door and hurried over to them, his expression grim. "How bad is it?"

"I don't know." Tears pricked her eyes and she gently pushed Cash over so he was on his back. There was blood congealed on his right shoulder.

She found his pulse, but it was faint and thready. She bowed her head, praying for God to spare Cash's life.

Please, Lord Jesus, please? Don't take Cash away from me!

Losing Cash was too high a price to pay in exchange for having Robbie arrested.

In the dim recesses of his mind, Cash heard voices. The words were indistinguishable, but when he was jostled, pain shot through him.

"Detective? We're taking you to the closest trauma center," a voice said.

He knew that he'd end up in Madison, at the large trauma center there. He groaned and tried to stay focused.

"Jacy?" Her name was little more than a croak.

"I'm here, Cash." Jacy's blurred face loomed above him. He belatedly realized he was being carried on a stretcher. His injuries must be worse than he'd realized. "Robbie has been arrested. It's over."

"Good." He wanted to say something reassuring, but he was having trouble staying awake. His eyelids were so heavy. "You."

"What did you say?" Jacy asked. "What about me?"

Had he spoken out loud? He struggled to bring her face into focus. To repeat the words.

I love you.

But darkness enveloped him before he could utter a sound.

The next thing he knew, he was in a hospital with blinding bright lights overhead. Beeping sounds and more muted voices reached his ears, but he couldn't see anything because of the lights.

Where was Jacy? Had she said something about Robbie no longer being a threat? Had Vargas arrested him?

And what about the three missing girls from ten years ago?

"Mr. Rawson? Can you hear me?" A man's face slowly came into focus. "I'm Doctor Harper. I'm the trauma surgeon on duty. I have an orthopedic surgeon on standby, and we're taking you to the operating room to repair the damage done by the two bullets that struck you."

Two bullets? He only remembered one. Well, except from the thigh wound where he'd only been grazed. "When?"

"Now." Dr. Harper looked concerned. "Waiting would add to the risk of infection, which is already bad enough with the dirt embedded in both wounds."

Okay, that was fair. He'd rolled on the dirty farm-house floor and the ground outside without paying attention to the grit, being more focused on stopping Robert White from hurting Jacy. "Can I talk to Jacy Urban? And Detective Vargas? Are they here?"

"I don't know who they are, but there could be people in the waiting room." The doctor glanced over and asked, "Wendy, is there someone waiting for this guy?"

"I'll check."

Cash hoped he hadn't sent someone on a wild-goose chase. The more he thought about it, the more he realized Vargas would likely have Jacy with him at the precinct, questioning her about the events that had unfolded at the farmhouse.

"Never mind," he mumbled. "Go ahead with the surgery, Doc."

"We're getting the OR prepped now," Harper said. "If there is someone in the waiting room, we'll let you see them before we go."

His eyes slid closed, an odd sense of disappointment washing over him. There was no reason to be upset about being there alone. The most important thing was that White was in custody.

Knowing the serial killer wouldn't hurt anyone else, ever again.

"I'm sorry, no one is in the waiting room for Mr. Rawson," a voice said apologetically. "I left a message for the volunteer to inform any visitors that Mr. Rawson is in surgery."

"Okay, let's get him to the OR, then." Dr. Harper's voice took on a businesslike tone. "Make sure that first dose of antibiotics has been infused before we go."

"It will be."

Cash was then pushed through hallways and taken by elevator to wherever the operating rooms were located. Another doctor in scrubs came and asked several questions about allergies to anesthesia or any other meds.

He answered to the best of his ability, since he'd never had surgery before.

Then there was nothing but darkness.

Cash woke to more medical staff leaning over his bed. He was confused at first, until he remembered being shot in the shoulder and thigh.

And undergoing surgery.

His shoulder ached, but the pain wasn't as bad as he'd anticipated. He tried to focus on the one doctor he recognized from earlier.

"Mr. Rawson? I'm Doctor Harper. You're in the recovery area. The surgery went well. Thankfully, the damage wasn't as bad as we feared. We washed both wounds with antibiotic solution. The flesh wound made by the bullet on your thigh has been left open. It should heal fine. We will need to watch the injury to your shoulder more closely."

Cash wasn't sure what that meant. A longer hospital stay? He swallowed a groan. He didn't want to hang around one minute longer than he had to.

Not that he was in a position to argue.

He wanted to ask if anyone was waiting to see him but decided against it. He had no idea how long the procedure had taken, but it didn't really matter.

Jacy was likely still tied up with being interviewed by Vargas. And if she was finished? That didn't mean she was planning to show up at the hospital. Hadn't she mentioned her car being in the repair shop? And with uncovering two dead bodies, Vargas wouldn't have time to give her a ride.

Maybe it was better this way. A clean break. His time with Jacy was over. She had her life to go back to, and he did, too. Granted, his injury and subsequent surgery meant he'd be stuck on desk duty for far longer than he'd like, but that wasn't the worst thing in the world.

He closed his eyes, doing his best to relax. Jacy was right about one thing, the danger was over.

Still, he wished he'd hear from Vargas about the other three missing women. Surely, Vargas would question White about them.

He highly doubted White would cooperate in sealing his fate on three more murders. Despite how their families had a right to know what had happened.

They deserved closure.

Time passed in spurts of consciousness. He assumed that when they gave him pain meds, he fell asleep, which was probably good for healing, but not great when he wanted to know what was going on.

He woke up for the third time in a private room. The pain was worse now, likely the reason he'd roused. When he shifted in the bed, a sharp ache shot through his shoulder up to his neck and down to his fingers.

Ignoring the pain, Cash took in his surroundings. An IV was connected to a tube in his arm and, craning his neck, he noticed there was a small monitor in the corner of the room displaying his heart rate. Based on the fact that he was alone, without a nurse hovering over him, he assumed his condition was stable.

Painful, but stable.

He didn't want more pain meds, better to have his mind clear. His brain was foggy enough from the effects of the anesthesia.

He patted his pockets for his cell phone, only to realize he was wearing a hospital gown. He vaguely remembered telling Jacy to use his phone to call 9-1-1.

Maybe she'd stop by to return it in person. He brightened at the thought.

On cue, the door to his room opened. His pulse jumped, the heart monitor beeping faster, but the newcomer was a nurse.

Not Jacy.

"Mr. Rawson, my name is Debra. I'm your nurse for the evening." She was cute, with dark hair and a sweet smile, but he preferred Jacy. "Would you like more pain medication?"

"No. Look, I need to call Detective Vargas, Dennis Vargas. He's with the Appleton Police Department." He pinned her with a serious glance. "Can you help me get the number?"

Debra frowned. "Mr. Rawson, you need to rest."

"I can't rest until I talk to him. We were chasing a murderer. I need to know what happened." He shifted on the bed, drawing in a sharp breath. "Please. I'll rest after I talk to him, okay?"

"I'll see what I can do," she reluctantly agreed. "But first I need to check your vital signs."

"Okay." He relaxed, trying to bring down his blood pressure and heart rate. No sense in setting off more alarms.

Debra finished up by checking his IV then making notes in the computer mounted in another corner of the room. He told himself Debra would come through for him, and when his door opened again fifteen minutes later, he looked over expectantly.

This time, Vargas himself entered the room. "You don't look so good, Rawson."

"Thanks," he muttered dryly. "I'm glad you're here. I need to know what happened with White. Did he confess to killing all five girls?"

"No, he's shut down all communication until his lawyer arrives." Vargas stepped closer, placing his small disposable phone next to him on the bed. "But it turns out he did confess to Jacy about killing Claire and Suzanna when they were at the farmhouse. And he mentioned Beth, too. Jacy gave a detailed account on everything that happened."

"He did?" Cash wished he could speak to Jacy himself. Where was she, anyway? If Vargas was here, he could have brought Jacy with him.

Unless she hadn't wanted to come.

"She endured a lot during the time White had her," Vargas said. "First he tased her, to get her away from the bridge. Then, when they arrived at the farmhouse, Jacy tried to run away. That time, he shot her with the dart gun."

"He drugged her?" Cash felt sick at what Jacy had gone through at White's hands.

"She managed to escape a third time by throwing a glass of water in his face." A smile tugged at Vargas's mouth. "Glass included. It slammed into the bridge of his nose."

"Good for her," Cash murmured. He had absolutely no sympathy for White. The guy deserved it. "I admit I was shocked when she came running out of the house. I'd taken the time to cut his tires to prevent him from escaping." He grimaced then added, "Although he still almost got away."

"He didn't," Vargas assured him. "He's here, getting treatment, too. I'll be escorting him back to jail as soon as he's cleared. His wounds aren't as bad as yours."

"Good to know." Cash opened his mouth to ask about Jacy when Vargas's phone rang.

The detective listened for a moment then said, "I'll be there ASAP, thanks." He put the phone in his pocket. "I have to go. White is being discharged. Here, I brought your phone so you could make calls as needed. I'll touch base with you again, Rawson. At some point, I'll need your full statement, too."

Without waiting for a response, Vargas left.

Cash stared at the door for several minutes after he'd gone.

There was still no sign of Jacy. And he couldn't help feeling dejected that she hadn't bothered to say goodbye.

SIXTEEN

Hiding a flash of impatience, Jacy smiled at her female witness as she turned the sketchpad toward her. She desperately wanted to get to Madison to see Cash but hadn't been able to turn down the request to help find another creepy guy who'd physically assaulted a young woman. Seeing the bruises darkening the girl's face from where he'd struck her while trying to grab her purse had made Jacy angry. But she didn't let on to her already-frightened-enough witness. "Amelia, how does this look?"

Amelia's eyes widened. "That's him! That's the man who hit me and tried to rob me!"

"I'm glad." Jacy shifted her eyes toward the Appleton police detective standing beside them as she carefully removed the sketch from her pad and handed it over. "Here you go. I hope this helps you find this guy and soon." She hesitated, adding, "If you don't need anything else, I have someplace I need to be."

"No, this is great. Thanks, Jacy." Detective Miles took the sketch. "I need a minute to scan this in and distribute it to all the officers in the area."

"Good." Jacy nodded in satisfaction.

The detective escorted Amelia out, taking the sketch with him. He returned a few minutes later. "All set. I understand you're looking for a ride?"

"Yes." She held his gaze. "Detective Vargas promised someone would take me to pick up my car as soon as I'd finished up here. It's been at the repair shop on Barker for the past few days." Days that had spanned a lifetime.

"He mentioned that to me." His eyes hardened. "Vargas just called to let me know he's at the farmhouse with a K-9 team specializing in cadaver searches. He's having the cop and the German shepherd canvass the entire property to see if they can find anything. He asked me to take you to the garage, since he can't."

Jacy's stomach rolled at the thought of a cadaver K-9 team searching for the missing girls. "I hope they find something," she murmured.

"Me, too." Detective Miles gestured toward the door. "Come with me. I have a squad car parked out front."

"Thanks." Her phone was still considered evidence, and Vargas had taken Cash's cell phone from her at the farmhouse, too.

Vargas had given her an update earlier through Miles, letting her know Cash was out of surgery and that his condition was stable. But that wasn't good enough.

She needed to see him for herself.

The car repair shop was still open and, thankfully, her car was ready. Jacy thanked Detective Miles, paid the car repair bill with her credit card and gratefully slipped behind the wheel.

Minutes later, she was driving on the interstate, toward Madison.

Shortly after Cash had been taken to the hospital, Vargas had insisted she return to Appleton to give her formal statement about how she'd been tased, kidnapped, escaped the truck, then shot with a tranquilizer dart and taken to the farmhouse, where she'd managed to escape, again.

Vargas also asked to have her blood drawn to see if any remnants of the drug Robbie had hit her with might still be in her system. Of course, she'd readily agreed, knowing that both activities were important in keeping Robbie behind bars.

But it all seemed to take way too much time. And when they'd finally finished, she'd been asked to do a sketch for a recent assault and attempted robbery.

Her sketchbook and pencils had been left in Cash's SUV, which the cops wanted held for evidence, so Detective Miles had run out to buy new supplies for her. That had caused another delay.

Turning her back on a woman who'd been assaulted with the intent to rob her had been impossible, so Jacy had worked with Amelia to do the sketch. It had only taken thirty minutes to complete that task. But driving to Madison would take another two hours.

Two hours!

Thankfully, traffic was light and she made decent time on the highway. She found herself glancing frequently at the rearview mirror, only to remember she wasn't in danger anymore.

Thanks to God's grace and Cash's keen instincts, Robbie wouldn't hurt anyone ever again.

When she finally reached the hospital, she parked in the visitor lot and hurried inside. Detective Vargas had told her what room Cash was in, so she didn't stop at the desk but made a beeline for the elevator.

On the fourth floor, the antiseptic scent made her wrinkle her nose. Every hospital she'd ever been in smelled the same. It reminded her of how she'd lost both parents to cancer.

Upon reaching Cash's room, her steps slowed. She didn't want to wake him if he was sleeping, but maybe she could sit in the room without disturbing him. She tapped lightly on the door.

"Come in," Cash answered in a hoarse voice.

She pushed open the door and stepped inside. Cash looked pale and tired in the hospital bed, making her heart squeeze with how close she'd come to losing him.

His eyes widened in surprise when he saw her. "Jacy? I'm surprised to see you."

He was? She stepped forward, closing the door behind her. "I'm sorry I didn't get here sooner."

"It's okay." He averted his gaze, as if he hadn't really cared if she was there or not. "I spoke to Vargas, sounds like White isn't talking."

She didn't really care about Robbie White now that he was in jail. She went over to stand near the edge of his bed. "How are you feeling, Cash? Vargas told me your surgery went off without a problem, but that you were in a lot of pain."

"Surgery hurts," he said wryly. His eyes searched hers for a moment. "I'm glad you're okay, Jacy. I know the time you spent with White must have been scary."

She told herself his preoccupation with Robbie was natural, considering the guy had shot him. She lightly touched Cash's arm. "I did my best to keep him talking, because I knew you'd find me."

"Almost too late," Cash muttered. He glanced down at her hand resting on his arm before looking up at her. "I guess you gave Vargas your statement?"

She nodded. "First, they took a vial of blood to test for remnants of the drug Robbie had used on me. Then I gave my statement, which took a long time because they kept asking more questions. Then, before I could leave, a Detective Miles asked me to do a sketch for a woman who was assaulted by a man who attempted to rob her." She sighed and added, "Once all of that was done, I had to get a ride to the garage to pick up my car. Then I made the two-hour drive to get here. Better late than never, right?"

"What?" Cash's eyes collided with hers. "They made you do a sketch after you'd been kidnapped, drugged and barely escaped a serial killer? What were they thinking?"

She arched a brow, taken aback by his response. "Maybe that I'm good at my job and that the perp who hurt that woman needs to be arrested and held responsible for his crime?" She didn't understand Cash's attitude. It was almost as if he resented her work for the police department.

Just like Greg had. Yet as soon as the thought entered her mind, she rejected it. No way. Comparing Cash to Greg wasn't fair. Cash would never cheat on his girlfriend, the way Greg had. Cash was an honorable and faithful man.

Still, she'd expected him to be supportive of her career.

She removed her hand from his arm and stepped back, feeling at a loss. Maybe coming here was a mistake. Her time with him was over. She was safe, and he needed time to heal from his wound. Just because she cared about Cash more than she should didn't mean he felt the same way.

Offering a tight smile, she said, "You're right about this being a long day, Cash. Probably the best and worst day of my life. I can't deny I'm exhausted. Yet I'm so thankful that Robbie is behind bars, where he belongs."

"Exactly my point," Cash said with a frown.

She went on, ignoring his comment, "But you, of all people, should understand that sketching suspects is what I do. It's not just a job, it's a calling. There was no way I was going to walk away from a victim who'd been brutally assaulted."

"I know but…" His voice trailed off. He rubbed his temple then said, "I'm sorry. Just ignore my bad temper. I thought you were avoiding me on purpose."

What? "Why would you think I'd avoid you? You saved my life, Cash. I owe you a debt of gratitude."

"I don't want your gratitude, Jacy." He held up his hand, so she stepped forward to take it, relaxing a bit as his warm fingers enclosed hers. "I want more."

More? She stared at him and then dropped her gaze to their joined hands. "You do?"

"Yes. I do." He gently squeezed her hands. "I know you may not be ready to hear this, but I've fallen in love with you, Jacy."

Love? She gave herself a mental shake. Was this for real? The last person who'd claimed to love her had cheated on her.

But Cash wasn't like that. He was the complete opposite of Greg Archer. In every single way except for being a cop.

"It's okay if you don't love me," Cash continued in a low voice. "I just wanted you to know."

She sank into the chair next to his bed, her knees going weak. Before she could say anything, though, her phone rang.

No, not her phone. She didn't have one. It was Cash's phone. He released her hand to answer it. "Rawson."

She watched as he listened to the caller. Then his somber look met hers. "Thanks, Vargas. Jacy is here with me. I'll let her know."

He set the phone on the bed, looking uncomfortable.

"Tell me what?" Jacy prodded.

"A K-9 cadaver team found the bodies of Emily, Beth and Kim at the abandoned farmhouse. Apparently, White used an area off in the distance, a hundred yards behind a half fallen-down barn, to bury his victims."

She closed her eyes and dropped her chin to her chest, silently praying the victim's families would experience a sense of peace and comfort.

Five murders. The man she'd once believed to be her friend had ruthlessly abducted and killed five innocent women.

The nightmare was over, now that Robbie was in jail. But at what cost? Knowing five young girls were dead made it difficult to be glad about that.

Especially since she was the one Robbie had wanted all along.

He hated seeing the distress filling Jacy's eyes. If his entire body didn't hurt so much, he'd have sat up in the bed, stood and gathered her into his arms.

But that wasn't possible. The most he could do was to cradle her hand in his, offering his support.

"I always suspected that they were dead," Jacy whispered. "If one or more had managed to escape, they'd have returned to their families."

"Yeah, I had the same thought." In some ways, he was glad they'd been found. "The other thing Vargas mentioned was that they found a stash of jewelry in a hidey-hole in the bedroom he'd been sleeping in. The same room where I found a police scanner. Trophy items he'd kept from each of his victims."

Her hand went to her neck and the crystal that hung there, as if imagining the necklace being in the hiding spot if he'd succeeded in killing her ten years ago. "That's good news, right? Those items will connect Robbie to each of the dead girls."

"Yes, that is very good news from a forensic standpoint." Cash had no doubt the case Vargas put together against Robert White would result in the man being put away for the rest of his life. "And as terrible as it is that the girls died, at least their families will know the truth. And they will be able to give those poor girls the proper burials they deserve."

"Yes, I'm sure that will help a little." After a long moment, her troubled eyes met his. "Why did God allow me to escape, Cash? Why am I alive while those poor girls are dead?"

He thought about that before he answered. This wasn't a question to take lightly. "You know I believe in God's plan. And that it's not up to us to question Him. But I think the reason you're alive now is because God knew all along that you would be the one to bring White to justice."

She opened her mouth as if she wanted to argue, but he stopped her.

"White might claim he killed those girls because he couldn't get to you, Jacy, but keep in mind, he's a brutal serial killer. If you ask me, he'd have killed other girls even if he'd succeeded in killing you first. A guy like that doesn't stop at one victim."

She was silent for a long moment then nodded slowly. "I think you're right about that. Robbie kept telling me that I didn't see him. That none of the pretty girls did, either. And then he admitted that it was only when he was strangling a girl that she truly saw him." Jacy shivered. "He wouldn't have stopped, Cash. Even if I was dead, he wouldn't have stopped."

"I completely agree with you on that," Cash murmured. "I'm just sorry that you had to be the one he focused on first."

"We were friends in school." She shook her head. "No, that's not right. I was friends with the boy I thought he was. The persona he portrayed to the world, not the killer he turned out to be. Looking back, the way he betrayed our friendship was a big factor in why I blocked the memories of that night." She held his gaze. "It was a dichotomy that didn't make sense. I truly cared about Robbie, but he would have killed me without blinking an eye. I guess I couldn't handle the truth."

"It's easy to understand that," he agreed. "And I don't blame you, Jacy."

"I still blame myself." She lifted a hand. "I know, you're going to say I'm not responsible. That what happened to those girls was wrong and evil, but it may have been part of God's plan that we were able to work together to stop Robbie from hurting anyone else."

"Yes, because that's true. You also need to remember

you were a scared sixteen-year-old girl. I highly doubt you'd judge other teenage girls as harshly as you're viewing yourself."

She sighed. "That's a fair point. But it's going to take some time to get over this."

Time and therapy, which might be good for her. "I'll support you in any way I can." His ill-timed declaration of love hung in the air between them. He now wished he'd kept his thoughts to himself. Then again, he didn't want her to walk away without knowing the truth. "You're not alone, Jacy. I'm here for you. No matter what you need."

A hint of a smile tugged at her mouth. "Thanks, Cash. I appreciate that."

He hesitated then decided he may as well go for it. "I hope you give me a chance to prove how much I care about you, Jacy. I know my timing isn't good, but I don't want to lose you. I hope we can see each other again once I'm discharged from the hospital."

Her expression softened. "Oh, Cash, I care about you, too. Staying away from the hospital to do the things I needed was very difficult. I wanted to be here sooner. To let you know that I'm here for you, too."

"I'm glad." He stared down at their clasped hands for a moment.

"I love you," Jacy said at the exact same moment he said, "I asked Vargas about positions in Appleton."

"What?" Jacy gaped at him. "You did?"

"You love me? Really?" He could barely believe what he was hearing.

She chuckled. "Yes, Cash, I love you. More than I could have thought possible. When you were lying on the ground outside the farmhouse, practically bleeding to death, I prayed God wouldn't take you away from me. That he would spare your life because I love you so much."

"I'm glad to hear that, because I love you. Being with you made me realize I didn't love Lana. Not the way I should have, to make that sort of commitment." Cash felt as if a huge weight had rolled off his chest. His shoulder still throbbed with pain but that didn't matter.

Jacy's love would get him through this. And his love would help her recover from what she'd endured at White's hands, too.

"I—uh, what did Vargas say about job openings?" Jacy asked hesitantly.

"He said there is a detective retiring at the end of May." Cash grimaced before adding, "I know that's a few months away, but I have a feeling I'll be off duty and relegated to a desk for at least twelve weeks. I want to be up to full speed before I take another position with the Appleton PD. If they'll have me." Vargas had promised to put in a good word for him, which might help.

And Cash knew his case closure rate was better than most, if he did say so himself.

"Are you sure?" Jacy's brow furrowed. "I support a lot of police precincts in the area, but I could consider relocating to Madison, if that's easier for you."

Her offer was heartwarming. "No, Jacy. I would never ask you to return to Madison." He suspected the city held too many bad memories. "I want you to be happy."

"I want you to be happy, too, Cash." She gave him an intense look. "I left Madison to escape the few memories I had, but I know now that I'll carry them with me regardless of where I live. And if moving to Madison is what you need, I'll make it work."

"Ah, Jacy. You're a sweetheart to make that offer. But, truthfully, I like Vargas and am looking forward to the opportunity to work with him." Her happiness was the most important thing to him. "I believe God brought us together there for a reason. Madison isn't a home, it's a place I've chosen to work. Home is where you are. And I like the thought of relocating to the Appleton area. Specifically, a place close to you."

"I'd like that, Cash," she admitted softly. "Very much."

"Good, then that's settled." He thought about mentioning she needed to consider a safer place to live, but decided that was a conversation for another day.

He didn't want to overwhelm her with his plans for their future. Best to take things one step at a time.

Besides, he wasn't even sure when he'd be able to get out of the hospital, much less move to Appleton. No point in charging ahead of himself.

"Jacy? I need one more favor." He groaned when he shifted in the bed. He might have to break down and take some pain meds. But not yet.

He wanted a clear mind for this.

"What's that?" Her gaze was full of concern. "Do you want a sip of water? Or should I get your nurse?"

"No. I need you to kiss me." He smiled and tugged on her hand. "Please? I love you, but I'm at a distinct disadvantage here. I can't get up out of bed to kiss you."

She laughed, the sound filling his heart with hope, joy and love. "Of course." She rose to her feet and leaned over the bed. "I love you, Cash Rawson," she whispered before kissing him.

He reveled in her warm embrace, even though it ended far too soon. Gazing into Jacy's twinkling eyes, he smiled, knowing her love was all he needed.

Now and until the end of time.

EPILOGUE

Four months later...

Jacy met Cash at his desk when she'd finished her sketch. She liked being able to stop in to see him when she was called in to work. And she'd been touched at how supportive Cash had been when it came to her driving miles away to do sketches for other police departments.

"Hey, beautiful." He rose and gave her a quick kiss. "I need about five more minutes, then we can bug out of here."

"Fine with me." She glanced over to where Vargas was working at the adjacent desk. Cash had been offered the job in Appleton before the date of the detective's retirement. Vargas had insisted on taking Cash on as his partner, and Cash had been thrilled at the opportunity to work with him.

His wound had healed well, without any nerve damage. She'd gone with Cash to the firing range and had been impressed with his accuracy. In her humble opinion, Vargas and Cash made a great team.

"Go ahead and get out of here, Rawson." Vargas

leaned back in his chair. "You'll be happy to know the Robert White case is officially closed."

"Closed?" Jacy glanced between Cash and Vargas. "How?"

"Let me guess, White pled guilty," Cash drawled.

"Yep. Even he was smart enough to realize the evidence stacked against him was impossible to overcome."

"That's great news," Jacy agreed. She hadn't been looking forward to testifying against Robbie at trial, but had been determined to make sure he paid for his crimes.

"I agree, this is good news." Cash nodded at Vargas. "Okay, if you're finished, too, I'll head out. See you Monday."

"Yep, have a good weekend," Vargas agreed.

Jacy knew both detectives had the weekend off, and she secretly hoped she wouldn't be called in to do any sketches, either.

She wasn't complaining but cherished the time alone she and Cash had. They'd joined a local church and she was thrilled to belong to its choir.

Cash had been incredibly supportive, watching her intently while she sang. She would never take him for granted.

"Shall we eat at Antonia's Italian restaurant for dinner?" Cash suggested. "I know it's your favorite."

"Sure." Normally they went there for special occasions. She supposed knowing Robbie had pled guilty to his crimes was something to celebrate.

Per Cash's suggestion, she'd met with a counselor for several weeks after the incident at the farmhouse. She was learning not to feel guilty over the loss of those five innocent girls. Dr. Barbra had convinced her to focus on how she'd helped bring a serial killer to justice.

When they arrived at the restaurant, she was surprised to realize Cash had called ahead to make a reservation. "Guess you were pretty certain I'd agree to come here for dinner," she teased as they were seated.

He grinned. "I was optimistically hopeful."

She didn't have to look at the menu for long. She knew her favorites. After they placed their order, Cash reached across the table to take her hand. "I love you," he said.

"I love you, too." Cash said those three little words often, and she never tired of hearing them.

"I have an idea of some things we can do this weekend." His gaze turned serious. "But first I have a question to ask."

"I'm open to your weekend plans, as long as you realize I might be called in to work."

"I know, that's fine." He reached into his pocket and pulled out a small velvet box. She gasped as he pushed it toward her. "Jacy, will you please marry me?"

"Oh, Cash." She didn't have to open the box to answer this question. "Yes! A thousand times, yes. I'd love to marry you."

"You didn't even look at the ring," he teased.

"I'm sure it's beautiful."

He smiled, stood and tugged her upright. He kissed her right there in the restaurant then turned to face the other patrons. "She said yes!"

"Cash, what are you doing?" Jacy hid her face against his chest as the restaurant burst into a round of applause.

"Hey, I have witnesses. You can't change your mind, now."

She laughed despite her keen embarrassment. "You're such a goofball. I'm not going to change my mind."

"Will you look at houses with me this weekend?" He turned and took the ring box off the table. He slid a beautiful diamond engagement ring on her finger. "Please?"

"Yes, Cash. We'll look for houses and we'll plan our future." She couldn't think of a better man to spend the rest of her life with.

And she had God to thank for bringing them together.

* * * * *

If you enjoyed this book, don't miss these other stories from Laura Scott:

Soldier's Christmas Secrets
Guarded by the Soldier
Wyoming Mountain Escape
Hiding His Holiday Witness
Rocky Mountain Standoff
Fugitive Hunt
Hiding in Plain Sight
Amish Holiday Vendetta
Deadly Amish Abduction
Tracked Through the Woods

Available now from Love Inspired Suspense!
Find more great reads at www.LoveInspired.com.

Dear Reader,

I hope you've enjoyed reading Jacy and Cash's story. I really wanted to give Jacy her own happily-ever-after. I have a great admiration for those who serve and protect their communities. Reading about a former victim turned forensic artist gave me the idea for this book. I hope you enjoyed it as much as I had fun writing it.

I'm hard at work outlining my next story. I think it's time for Chief Deputy Garrett Nichols to fall in love. What do you think?

I adore hearing from my readers! I can be found through my website at https://www.laurascottbooks.com, via Facebook at https://www.facebook.com/LauraScottBooks, Instagram at https://www.instagram.com/laurascottbooks/, and Twitter https://twitter.com/laurascottbooks. Also, take a moment to sign up for my monthly newsletter, to learn about my new book releases. (Like Garrett's story!) All subscribers receive a free novella not available for purchase on any platform.

Until next time,
Laura Scott

Get 3 FREE REWARDS!

We'll send you 2 FREE Books plus a FREE Mystery Gift.

FREE
Value Over
$20

Both the **Love Inspired®** and **Love Inspired® Suspense** series feature compelling novels filled with inspirational romance, faith, forgiveness and hope.

YES! Please send me 2 FREE novels from the Love Inspired or Love Inspired Suspense series and my FREE gift (gift is worth about $10 retail). After receiving them, if I don't wish to receive any more books, I can return the shipping statement marked "cancel." If I don't cancel, I will receive 6 brand-new Love Inspired Larger-Print books or Love Inspired Suspense Larger-Print books every month and be billed just $6.49 each in the U.S. or $6.74 each in Canada. That is a savings of at least 16% off the cover price. It's quite a bargain! Shipping and handling is just 50¢ per book in the U.S. and $1.25 per book in Canada.* I understand that accepting the 2 free books and gift places me under no obligation to buy anything. I can always return a shipment and cancel at any time by calling the number below. The free books and gift are mine to keep no matter what I decide.

Choose one: ☐ **Love Inspired Larger-Print**
(122/322 BPA GRPA)

☐ **Love Inspired Suspense Larger-Print**
(107/307 BPA GRPA)

☐ **Or Try Both!**
(122/322 & 107/307 BPA GRRP)

Name (please print)

Address   Apt. #

City   State/Province   Zip/Postal Code

Email: Please check this box ☐ if you would like to receive newsletters and promotional emails from Harlequin Enterprises ULC and its affiliates. You can unsubscribe anytime.

Mail to the Harlequin Reader Service:
IN U.S.A.: P.O. Box 1341, Buffalo, NY 14240-8531
IN CANADA: P.O. Box 603, Fort Erie, Ontario L2A 5X3

Want to try 2 free books from another series! Call **1-800-873-8635** or visit www.ReaderService.com.

---

*Terms and prices subject to change without notice. Prices do not include sales taxes, which will be charged (if applicable) based on your state or country of residence. Canadian residents will be charged applicable taxes. Offer not valid in Quebec. This offer is limited to one order per household. Books received may not be as shown. Not valid for current subscribers to the Love Inspired or Love Inspired Suspense series. All orders subject to approval. Credit or debit balances in a customer's account(s) may be offset by any other outstanding balance owed by or to the customer. Please allow 4 to 6 weeks for delivery. Offer available while quantities last.

Your Privacy—Your information is being collected by Harlequin Enterprises ULC, operating as Harlequin Reader Service. For a complete summary of the information we collect, how we use this information and to whom it is disclosed, please visit our privacy notice located at corporate.harlequin.com/privacy-notice. From time to time we may also exchange your personal information with reputable third parties. If you wish to opt out of this sharing of your personal information, please visit readerservice.com/consumerchoice or call 1-800-873-8635. **Notice to California Residents**—Under California law, you have specific rights to control and access your data. For more information on these rights and how to exercise them, visit corporate.harlequin.com/california-privacy.

LIRLIS23